*Hunted A Fight For Survival
By Abigail Swainston*

Hunted's playlist

- Everybody wants to rule the world- Lorde
- Control -Halsey
- Can you feel my heart- Bring me the horizon
- Radioactive – Imagine dragons
- War of Hearts – Ruelle
- Centuries- Fall out Boy
- Wicked Games – RAIGN
- Little Talks- Of Monsters And Men
- Chasing Cars- Snow patrol
- Team- Lorde

To the people who look at books to escape from reality

Prologue

Our world isn't like yours.

On your first birthday, they infused you with either a blue or purple serum. Even the person administering the shot cannot specify which it will be. On your seventh birthday, you learned to recognize which colour your tattoo would turn. If they gave you the blue antibody, three patterned blue swirls appear on your left wrist. If, but, you were unlucky to have gotten the purple serum, a purple skull shows up on your left wrist.

The skull means you've got a target on you for the rest of your life. The swirl means you are independent. Most Blues become guards, hunting their purple counterparts. Blues gets harsher precedents to observe, but they can lead their lives without fearing for it. Upon approaching the age 14, Blues learn to choose their prospect. Almost all Blues chooses to become guards living their lives in an unending game of cat and mouse. If you are a guard, your duty is to hunt and capture Purples for the King. Purples are killed on sight or taken to The Gaol. Purples aren't hunted until they mature, but many never meet their 18th birthday. This system was devised to control the population, but it's been over one hundred years.

The King's Great Ancestor established the perilous concept. Juveniles who's barely lived are being hunted. Most won't live a night after their eighteenth birthday, and that's the dark truth of our world. The point you turned eighteen, you are murdered or become a killer.

CHAPTER 1

HOME SWEET HOME

"Today is the day I risk my life for food."

Lila laughed. She wasn't lying. Her agenda was to go to the market and leave unnoticed, which would be quite difficult.

The smell of freshly cut grass and heather was the smell that hit when you entered the market

Lila was always an odd one out who hated standing out in the crowd. She was different in every way and never truly knew why. Having the purple skull on her wrist, made matters worse, but still wasn't the main reason. Others had the skull too. Lila had a striking appearance. Her eyes seem not to match. The left was an emerald, green color, and the right as blue as the sky. She never really liked them much until her parents were gone. Her mother had emerald, green eyes and her father had ice-blue eyes. Now she imagines she can see the world through their eyes.

Her journey through life has taken several courses over the past few years. At only 14, she became the only one the blues feared. They never got a glance at her face. She killed people who were born to kill and saved those who were born to die. It wasn't until they killed her younger brother, she realized she was fighting a losing battle all along. She gave up and moved away from the major cities to draw less attention to herself, headed for the lost forest, far away from any civilization. Growing up, Lila detest the fact that she would become purple, but it was inevitable given its hereditary nature.

Her mirror was cracked down the middle. If her mother was still alive, she would say that it was bad luck, but Lila never believed in that stuff.

The snow was an untouched blanket around the trees. The city is not much different from any other city under the king's rule. There are two cities free from his reign, but no map lists them.

"*More hidden than me,*" Lila chuckled.

The forest looks like a dream, but the reality is nothing like it. No, instead, it's more like an insidious nightmare that you can't fully wake up from. With time, you can get used to anything, even the very worst of things.

After six hours of walking, Lila reached the end of the forest. When she arrived, it was around twelve o'clock in the afternoon. The buildings were hardly standing; the streets filled with litter, bricks, and wood. Smashed windows and broken shelters. This used to be the place where most purples would take shelter. Now it's a place of deathly silence.

There are only two things that can kill you

The unknown and the uncertainty.

Lila stood there in brief silence. She was heartbroken over the killings and torture going on in the kingdom. People were starting to notice her. Quickly, she wiped her tears and walked over to the crowd, trying to blend in. She watched as a few people were dragged into murderous vans and hated feeling helpless; at the same time thinking of ways to save them, without endangering herself. The market was quite busy, the king's guards were everywhere, and the queues looked endless. She must've stood in the line for two hours. Getting closer to the front, she observed they were checking for marks. Not having worn any, she panicked but couldn't leave. It would look suspicious. "There's no way I'm going to make it out of here alive," she said to herself.

A guard walked up to her as she reached the front. There were many people behind her and there were guards at every angle. "Nowhere to run," she thought to herself.

"Arm." The guard demanded. He could tell she was hesitant as Lila rolled her sleeve up. A gun shot was heard nearby causing the guards to sprint towards the noise. People scrambled in every direction. She was left alone. Lila ran to the other side of the counter, alone, thinking she was alone until she heard one of the scales drop. She spun around. A thief. The Thief had short messy brown hair with a faint scar going through his left eyebrow. His left eye had an unusual faint scar going through it. He had filled his bag with many goods. She turned back around and grabbed the last loaf of bread and packed it in her bag.

She placed two gold coins on the counter. Lila was anything but a thief. Most people would keep their money and run, but Lila knew that if she did, the workers would be castigated. Usually that puts people off stealing, but not this thief. He just didn't care. Then again, why should he? They took his freedom away, so why shouldn't he?

"You will not keep that?" The thief asked as he pointed at the money. "There's a lot more food over here if you want any".

She walked back and took the last jar of jam, adding another coin to the counter. They could both hear the guards rushing back over. It happened so quickly that Lila was still wondering how they ended up hiding underneath one of the counters. They could hear voices, but neither of them could make out any of the words. They both pulled the cloth down to make an instant hideaway. There was a small crack on the wooden counter. Lila watched as everything went back to normal just like clockwork. Not a single soul mentioned the gunshots, almost as if it never happened at all.

"What are we going to do now?" Lila asked the thief. He looked at her with confusion. He had been in a lot of situations, but nothing similar to this. He was supposed to get the food and return to Blake, but he lost track of time and ended up in this mess.

"No clue." The thief whispered. The worker placed her hand through the cloth and they both held their breath until the thief pointed to something.

Lila looked at him, confused, with no idea what he was pointing at. For all she knew, he was pointing at her to run.

"The box behind you," He hissed. She then pushed the small box into the woman's hand and the woman stood up again. She didn't see either of them. Lila sighed in relief; they both knew they were going to be here for a while. Many scenarios entered their minds, but none were a sure bet to get out alive. It then came to the thief that he didn't know what mark the girl had. Without hesitation, he grabbed her arm. Lila panicked until he said "Same as mine", revealing the purple skull on his wrist. They sat in silence for what felt like forever.

"When the workers leave, we have about two minutes until their break ends, which leaves us about a minute to leave," Lila whispered to the thief. He thought about it for a few minutes. There was still a risk but less of a risk with this plan.

The worst thing possible happened: his phone went off.

The thief searched his pockets and his bag. He quickly turned it off and placed his hand over his mouth.

"Did you hear that?" The woman asked. Lila and the thief' held their breath in sheer terror.

"Hear what?" One of the workers questioned.

"Nothing," the woman replied.

The thief sighed in relief. Lila looked through the crack in the counter and there seemed to be more guards appearing. She watched in horror as people were dragged into vans before her eyes; it shocked her anytime she watched someone being dragged away, knowing they will never escape.

Lila sat in silence, covering her ears to block out the screams of people who were being taken. The thief thought that was a close call. Lila just wanted to smash his bloody phone.

An hour passed, and the workers left again, but the guards were still there.

"Do you trust me?" The thief asked.

"No," she answered confidentially.

"Good," He said. Without a warning, he grabbed Lila's hand, and they both scrambled through the white sheet that was keeping the back of the market unseen. Lila glanced back to see that they had caught the eye of some guards, so they both started running. She had no clue where they were running to and the guards were closing in rapidly.

They stopped running when they reached an alley. It was a dead end. The abandoned buildings were boarded with wood and the lights dangling were flickering on and off. There were two barrels on either side of the alley. Without clearly thinking, they hid behind them.

There was an eerie silence between them. The thief prayed that neither of them would get caught. Lila thought about her family and how they were killed. She would never forget what her parent's killer looked like. Her parents had built a safety room, but there was a tiny crack in one wall which she could see out of. Her brother was also in the safety room, but luckily for her, he was asleep when her parents were being killed. She lost track of what was happening until the thief ran over to her.

"I think we lost them," the thief gasped, still trying to catch his breath.

"Pass me your phone," Lila asked the thief. He was hesitant, but then passed her. She immediately threw it to the ground, the screen smashing on the hard concrete.

"What was that for?" He shouted at her.

"This thing almost got us killed." Lila said while clenching her teeth in anger.

The thief was furious with the girl, but he said nothing.

"So, what's your name, thief?" Lila said, trying to change the subject that hadn't come up yet.

"Greyson, and you are," the thief replied. Before the girl could say anything, an unknown person stood up on one of the buildings. Greyson turned around to his disappointment it was not who he was waiting for.

"Who are you?" Greyson said, trying to sound imposing. The hooded figure didn't move. Greyson looked back at Lila, who was just as confused as him. It only became clear when they could hear running. It was a trap. Greyson's mind flooded with questions.

Greyson looked at Lila as if he was trying to tell her something, but he should have learnt from before that she's not good with signs.

"Just run," He whispered, trying not to draw too much attention to them. Lila jumped over the wall and sprinted up the stairs on one of the other buildings. As she ran up the stairs, guilt slowly filled her mind. A second before Greyson was taken, he looked up at her before he disappeared into the van. He didn't look scared, but then again, he might have just been that good at hiding it.

She had no idea what to do. Instead stayed hidden on the top of the building and watched the van drive off. She knew what they would do to him. They would torture him for information, but since he knew nothing about her, not even her name, he would definitely suffer. Lila looked up at the sky and watched the sunset, but it couldn't take her mind off the thief and how he saved her.

She looked back down at the alley to see a person appear. He had short jet-black hair and his arms covered in tattoos.

"Gray... where are you?" The stranger asked. The world stayed silent. Lila picked her bag off the floor but one of her knives fell out of the bag and onto the ground not far from the stranger. His eyes shot up, but she quickly hid behind the building. Lila glanced back down at the stranger. He waited for his friend who Lila knew wasn't returning.

"He was taken. I would run if I were you." She shouted from behind the other building. He disappeared and Lila did the same. It was dark outside and there was no way she would make it back home. When the clock hits 12, the guards don't care if you're a blue or purple. You would be shot in sight. It was only half nine, but she didn't want to chance it. Lila passed a few people in the street but had no clue where she was going to sleep. She came across a dilapidated street. The houses all looked like they were falling or would collapse if you set one foot inside. All but one. It was destroyed, but it looked stable enough. There were a few chipped stone steps leading to the house. The door was hardly attached to the crooked door frame. Lila walked into the house. There was an old mattress lying in the middle of the floor. She hardly ever gets enough sleep. She was so tired she didn't even remember drifting off.

CHAPTER 2

BREATHING IS SURVIVING

Earlier that morning in a different part of the city

Melanie and Noah entered. It's around 4 'o'clock in the morning now. Melanie is accustomed to not sleeping much. She glances at her brother, who is still fast asleep. Melanie is only twelve, but she is nine-year-old and Noah's only caregiver. They are both purples. Melanie likes to believe that they are orphans, but deep down, she knows her father is out there somewhere. Her mother was a purple, but her father was a die-hard blue. When he found out about her mark, he killed her in cold blood. But what he didn't know is that his children were both purples. Melanie left with her brother and never told him what had happened. Their father is one of the king's most trusted guards. She doesn't keep many secrets from Noah, but she will die before she tells him the truth about their parents.

The only two rooms in the house that weren't overly destroyed were Noah's room and the kitchen. Melanie was always slightly jealous about Noah's room because it was silver and not falling apart. Melanie's room looked like it had been to hell and back. When they were little, people found it so hard to believe that they are family. Since Melanie had long brown hair with brown eyes, she was a spitting double of her mother. Her brother had blonde hair with brown eyes. If Noah was older, he could literally be their father's twin. They had little to survive on since they were only children. They had a few clothes and just enough food for the both of them.

Melanie opened one cupboard to reveal a bit of porridge left and a loaf of bread. The floorboards creaked, and she realized her brother was awake.

"Did you have a good sleep?" She asked her brother.

"Not bad." It felt as if he knew something was off.

Melanie wanted him to fear the world, because fear comes with caution, and caution comes with safety.

"Don't worry about me. We are going to be fine." Noah says.

Melanie thought it was unlikely that they would be fine.

"Yeah, you're probably right. Come, eat". The girl placed a bowl of porridge on the counter. He ate like there was no tomorrow. His eyes scanned the kitchen.

"You cleaned." He sounded surprised.

"Yeah, I know for once I had time to clean the kitchen." Melanie hardly ever has time to clean the kitchen or do anything else.

" Are you feeling alright" Noah said sarcastically.

"Hilarious." Melanie laughed.

I have to go. Do you remember what to do in case I don't come back? Melanie asked nonchalantly. Noah hated being reminded.

Yes, if you're not back by midnight, leave the house and get away from the major city."

" Don't forget I love you Noah." She quickly hugged him; she knows she will be back.

" Love you too Mel," He says smiling as he watches her leave.

As she walked outside, she placed her hood over her head to keep out of sight. The street deserted. The king's guards surrounded the crowds, which makes her situation more of a risk, but possible. There are a few markets around here, but the biggest one is also the cheapest. Technically, Melanie doesn't own any money, though she's a talented pick pocket who never thought the act was truly stealing, more like borrowing and never returning.

As she gets to the front of the queue, she saw the guards chasing two young people. Most likely purples. A lot of the guards went to see what the commotion was, but a few stayed back. Luckily for Melanie, the guards were too busy capturing the people. As she gets to the front of the queue, an old worker with brown curly hair summons her over.

Melanie begins to say, "Can I buy one pou-"

"You should be more careful, child. You may think you're unnoticeable, but with your hood over your head you're even more obvious." She whispered, quiet enough that she could have been a voice in Melanie's head. Melanie quickly pulled her hood down to reveal her messy plated hair.

"Are you that dumb to come out here? They could kill you without a breath. What are you 10?" Speaking again as if there was no sound coming out of her mouth.

"I'm 12 actually, thanks for-"

"Don't thank me for not reporting you. Don't waste your breath, kid." She then handed Melanie two packed bags.

"Twenty -six gold pieces," she exclaims. Melanie didn't know what was happening.

"But I don't have that much money." Melanie spoke in a faint tone.

The quiet woman mumbled, "On the house again, don't thank me." Melanie had nowhere near the amount of money for this. The strange woman then called the next person; Melanie walked the long way instead of risking it again. She walked past several guards, but was preoccupied trying to find the two runners.

Melanie looked towards the end of the street there was over twenty guards searching for the runners. She slowly turned around to avoid them. But there was one standing behind her. He towered over the girl. There was no way she could escape. The guards were all wearing black bulletproof suits that covered their entire body, including their face. One guard went to grab her arm, but she kept moving backwards. Then she was surrounded and she couldn't move any further away.

"Arm," one guard commanded. Even though she couldn't see their eyes, she could feel them all watching her. One of them stepped closer to her. She knew they would not wait much longer. She looked up at one building, which had a massive clock attached to the side. It was almost half eleven Melanie hoped her brother follows the rules and leave the minute it hits midnight. She sat against the wall and closed her eyes. She knew they would kill her there and then, because what useful information could a twelve-year-old possibly have.

She heard screams. She couldn't tell if she was dead or not, but just stayed sitting with her hands on her ears.

"You're okay, you can open your eyes" Melanie recognized the voice and did as the stranger told.

CHAPTER 3

FLASHBACK FROM TWO YEARS AGO

Melanie's POV

Blake Hunter. The only reason I'm still alive is because the day my mark appeared, my mother took me to see a person called Blake Hunter. He was only sixteen when I met him; he was also a purple. He lived in the same house as I did. You would think that they would eventually realize over time, but they didn't suspect a thing until my mother. There was only one way to get rid of the purple mark, which was to get the blue mark transferred on top, but it doesn't last forever and it was painful. I didn't see Blake that much after, not until I was ten. He did the same thing for Noah. He spent quite a lot of time with Noah.

The day Melanie and Noah's mother were killed.

I couldn't sleep at all, so when the sun rose, I got out of bed. I could hear my father on the phone in his office. Nobody could ever go in there other than my father, not even my mother.

Noah was still asleep. Since my father is one of the king's best men, we live in the best part of the city. There's a wall surrounding the palace, the 'Gaol' and the mansion I live in. We share the mansion with the Hunters. Hardly do I see the other families. They're almost never inside. Ensuring to live far away from them, if they knew I wasn't a blue, they'd kill me in a second. I could hear arguing coming from the office. The voices were my mother and father, which was weird because no one's allowed in there.

I heard my mother cry and wish I had walked in there. Maybe I could've stopped him, but the last words I heard from him were "What would they do to me if they found out my wife was one of them." One gunshot and then silence. That was when I realized that he never cared for anyone other than himself and his position in society. I ran to Noah's room to get him out before the other hunters try killing us. I sprinted into his room, grabbed a random bag, and packed it for him. Somehow, he was still asleep. The gunshot hadn't woken him from his slumber. I ran to him and woke him. It was only five in the morning. They wouldn't expect us to be up for another hour. I had no clue what to say to Noah. The only thing I knew was that we might not make it out alive on our own. Noah's room was on the ground floor, so if anything happened, he could run out the window.

"They found out about mom" I whispered to him. I was on the verge of tears, but I knew I didn't have time to cry.

"How? Is she… dead" I looked at him and I didn't know how to break it to him.

"She's dead. I think it was one of the Hunter's" I said. A little white lie won't hurt. The Hunters have killed hundreds of our kind, but if they found out about their son, they would kill him in a heartbeat. They had seven children all together. I never really talked to them, only Blake. I knew they deeply hated me because of my father, but they never dared to show it.

Noah and I wouldn't last a day on our own. We have to escape the mansion and somehow get through the wall.

"I have to go talk to Blake. I will be back in twenty minutes. If anyone walks in, pretend you're asleep. If that doesn't work, climb out the window and hide in the blade." The blade was our secret hideout we created when we were little. Nobody else knew about it other than us.

I walked out the door and check twice that no one was lurking around in the corridors to jump out and kill me. But everything seemed normal. Too normal.

Blake's room had to be on the other side of the mansion. The Hunter's end of the mansion was always quite dull. I would only ever come here to read. Next to the staircase, there was a painted family portrait of the hunters, which was set in a highly decorative golden frame that had 'the hunter family' etched into it. The smiles looked so forced. You could tell they were all miserable. Why should I care if they're miserable? They kill about ten innocent people a day. They're the veritable monsters. The only one of them that has killed no one is Blake.

I trudge up the staircase, trying not to make a sound even though they were the creakiest stairs in the entire place.

"What are you doing?" Blake asks loudly. I quickly turned to shush him, but his mother, Andrea Hunter, was standing at the top of the staircase and she looked furious. Blake looked nothing like his mother. She had light brown skin with long brown gorgeous hair. She was a beautiful woman with an ugly personality. Blake looked like his father. He had his jet-black hair and piercing blue eyes.

"What is going on here" She shouted at us both. I looked back at Blake, who just stood there.

"I came to ask Blake for some help with my history homework." I said calmly. We didn't go to school. We had home schooling, but we sadly still got given homework. Andrea walked back up the stairs.

"What history homework do you need help with?" he exclaimed, then he added in a quiet tone, "Now what do you really need? I shouldn't have to add another tattoo for at least another week."

"They know" I whispered. The two words can change anyone's mood. Blake looked terrified.

"What... what do you mean 'they know'?" He mumbled.

"What do you think it means" I hissed at him and added, "We need to get out of here, you me and Noah" I tugged at his arm and we ran down to Noah's room. If they knew we were awake, they could send someone to kill us this second. We quickly ran to my room and packed a bag. In case of emergencies, my mother kept two backpacks in my room. One of them was for Blake and the other, filled with weapons and things to help keep us alive.

We ran up to Noah's room, and I quickly unlocked the door. Theo Hunter stood with a knife to my brother's throat. It felt like my heart had stopped.

"Oh, brother, how I hoped it wasn't true. I guess I'm going to have to kill all of you." Theo said enthusiastically. "I have to admit, it doesn't bother me with the thought of killing you." Theo was psychotic.

Theo and Blake were twins, but looked quite different. Theo was a splitting double of his mother other than he had hazel eyes like their younger sister, Angela, and also had a slight gap in between his two front teeth.

I couldn't move and I was struggling to breathe, imagining the awful horrors that awaited us

I pleaded, "Please… Theo, don't kill him."

Blake threw a knife that pierced Theo's leg. Theo release Noah and collapsed to the floor. It all happened so fast. I could see Andrea and Maxwell Hunter running down the stairs, so I barricaded the door shut to buy us some time and quickly grabbed one of Noah's old English text books and threw it at the window, which caused it to shatter.

Noah whispered " lets get out of here," while climbing out of the window. I heard one hunter saying, Hurry! How long does it take to kick down a door?

Blake climbed through the window, and we started running. There were several exits out of the center, but they were all heavily guarded. In about five minutes, they would share a photo of us giving them clues what we look like and we will officially be tagged 'Wanted'.

We stopped when we reached the edge of the center.

"Have you ever been to the old warehouse?" Blake asked. I nodded. "There's a small gap to jump and then we have rope to climb down the other side, but we have to be quick, otherwise the guards will be alerted."

"Let's get going then." I spoke. Noah was only going to slow us down again, so Blake carried him.

When we reached the warehouse, I had to sit for a minute to catch my breath. Blake and Noah climbed the stairs to the top of the warehouse. I could hear them shout at me, so I started walking up the stairs. When I reached the top, I looked straight down. There was a massive drop, and it wasn't a small gap.

I looked straight at Blake. He already knew what I was going to say "You call that a small drop." I said under my breath.

Blake ran and jumped onto the wall with Noah on his back. He then placed Noah on the wall.

"Trust me and don't look down." He called.

I walked to the other side of the warehouse rooftop and counted to three.

One, Two, three. I ran. I wished I could just go back home, but I have no home now. Luckily, I made it. I grabbed onto the wall and pulled myself up.

The wall was quite narrow and, in some places, quite unstable. The wall is over five hundred years old and it crumbling away. I have always hated heights.

Blake quickly got the rope out of his bag. He attached it to the wall, but it still felt unstable.

"Tie this around your waist," He said while handing me the rope. He then added, "I'll quickly lower you down and then wait at the bottom for us." I nodded. I didn't want to look down when we were so high up. The boys soon followed. They were quick coming down.

"We need to leave quickly. I heard the alarm go off when we were climbing down."

We found a house in the quietest street ever. Blake made up the rule. If he was not back by midnight, we would have to leave. For a while, that never happened. Until one day I and Blake were out getting food supplies and the worst thing imaginable took place. He was caught and dragged into one of the guard's vans.

I vowed that day that I would never leave my brother, I would always try my best to get back to him.

I always assumed Blake Hunter was dead.

Chapter 4

Back to Present Time

Back again

Well, that was until today, Melanie thought. She looked up to see the person who had protected her since she was seven. He wasn't her brother by blood, but he was her brother as far as she knows.

She jumped up and hugged him.

"Hey Kid, it's been a while." He said while hugging her back.

"How are you still alive…? How did they not kill you…? How did you escape?" Melanie spoke rapidly.

"It's a long story. Is Noah still alive" Melanie nodded. He then added, "We better go see him then," He spoke while changing the subject.

Melanie knew Blake was hiding something, but she was too excited that he was back, so she didn't think too much about it. When they got back to the house, they both had this dreadful feeling that something terrible was waiting around the corner.

"I think Noah went to sleep," Melanie whispered to Blake. "There is a spare room. It's not perfect, but it will do."

They both slowly walk up the stairs to try not to wake Noah up. The door creaks open and a beam of light peeps through, barely penetrating the solid darkness of the room. Melanie walks in and even after two years of living in the house, she can't find the light switch. She felt something on her shoulder and spun around "Christ! Noah, you scared us," Melanie panicked. The boy just stood there, which was surprising since he had just found out that Blake was alive.

"Be quiet" He begged his sister.

She turned back around to try find the light switch she finally switched it on. She heard Blake gasp so she spun around to see a girl, she was tied up Blake turned around to face Noah

"What happened" He asked calmly.

"She snuck in the house. I didn't know what to do. She could have been sent to kill us. What if the hunters sent her?" Noah blurted out.

Melanie could feel Blake's eyes glaring at her.

"Noah, go to sleep. We'll be fine." Blake whispered to him.

As soon as he left, Blake's facial expressions changed. He then said in an angered tone, "What does he mean if the Hunter's sent them? Did you not tell him the truth?"

"Keep your voice down," Melanie spoke in a hushed tone. "I couldn't tell him. He had just lost his mother. My mind was all over the place. How was I going to tell him that his mother was killed by his father?"

"I understand why you didn't tell him, but you know you will have to tell him eventually."

Hopefully not soon, Melanie thought.

He then adds "What are we going to do about her" He said, pointing at the ginger girl who was tied to a rotted headboard.

Melanie shrugged her shoulders, not having a clue what to do with her.

"She should be awake by tomorrow, so I will stay in the room in case she tries to escape. Try to get some sleep." Melanie nodded and walked along the corridor to her room. She hadn't had a good night's sleep in two years, but for once she fell asleep quickly.

CHAPTER 5

WHO IS SHE?

Blake stayed awake all night in the silent room. The girl didn't wake up. In fact, it didn't even sound like she was breathing. Blake checked to make sure she was alright multiple times; she could have been sent here to kill them, but she could also have just wandered in here on her own. They had checked her wrists at ages ago, but neither of them had a mark, so they kept her tied up overnight.

It was morning already, and Blake was quite exhausted. Noah came rushing in to hug him. He felt better knowing that Blake was there to protect him. Melanie walked in about an hour later. For once, she looked like she slept well.

Melanie had already made some toast with jam and butter. It was quite lucky for them both, since they hardly ever had enough food for just the two of them. But because of the strange women's kindness, they had enough food to feed the three of them for at least a month. Melanie always stored some cans of food away, just in case they ever ran out.

"Do you think she will wake up soon?" Noah asked Blake.

"I don't know. Let's hope she wasn't sent to kill us," Blake spoke bluntly.

The girl was awake, but her eyes tightly shut. Melanie looked at the girl again and she noticed she seemed to adjust.

Melanie walked back over to Blake and whispered, "I think she might already be awake."

"We know you're awake. We won't hurt you." She promised the stranger. Blake added, "Unless you give us a reason, too."

The stranger's clear blue eyes shot open.

"I'm a purple in case you're wondering," the stranger confessed.

"Who are you?" Melanie questioned the girl.

"Lila, Lila Wood, age seventeen," she answered. Blake took the kids out into the hall. Lila could hardly make out what they were saying, but they said something about 'kill her.' Lila never got afraid of dying, the only thing that bothered her was about leaving the world doing nothing to save the people.

She tried to untie her hands, but they seemed to dig into her skin. Blake walked back in alone.

"I don't believe you. Who sent you?" He shouted at Lila. She recognized the person, but she didn't know where from. Took a glance at his arms. They were both covered in tattoos. She quite liked them. There were a few symbols and then there were a few names. Melanie, Noah, Isabella and Greyson. Greyson, she thought. He was the boy who was shouting Grey in the alley.

"Greyson. You're the boy in the alley shouting of your friend, aren't you?" She calmly asked Blake.

"You're the girl on top of the building. Aren't you?" He muttered.

He walked back out of the room, which left Lila to her thoughts.

Melanie walked in with a bowl of porridge. She placed the bowl on the dusty stand next to the bed. Lila thought to herself, 'this is torture'.

"If you tell me how you know Greyson, I will give you the food." Melanie stated.

"How do you know the thief" Lila questioned Melanie.

Melanie seemed confused because Lila had referred to Greyson as 'The thief. Mel had never actually met Greyson. She just wanted to hear what he was like but knew that Blake and Greyson were best friends and she had been told lots of things about him, but she wanted to know more. She knew Greyson had saved many people. He had saved Alec from 'The Gaol' once or twice. When Blake was first captured and taken to 'The Gaol', Melanie and Noah left like he told them to do. When Blake finally escaped with Greyson, who was captured with him, the first thing they did was try to find Melanie and Noah. A mission that was unsuccessful, and ended up getting themselves taken again.

"He's my cousin," Melanie lied. Lila knew she was lying, but she was starving and could not reach her bag, that had her food supplies for the next fortnight. So, she told her about how she caught him stealing and how they hid under the counter and how he was taken.

"He will be alright you know he has escaped that hell hole twice. Don't tell Blake that you told me about him." Blake must be the boy with the tattoos on his arm Lila assumed. Mel then untied one of

Lila's hands so she could eat. She passed the bowl to Lila, and she walked back out of the room.

It didn't feel like she had been in the room for long, but it was already getting dark outside.

A deafening sound started playing from outside. The children sprinted into the room. Noah was on the verge of tears and Melanie was as pale as a ghost. Lila could hear Blake sprinting up the stairs. He was panicking.

It had been 2 years since Lila had heard that deadly intro. It used to give her a chance to either save or kill someone. Melanie and Noah had never heard the intro to the murder night. For Blake, it felt like another lifetime ago. Murder night was the music that was played before the guards would go on a rampage to find the hidden purples. It rarely ever happens because the king thinks the majority of them are dead, but he's definitely wrong. Today had been more off than usual she watched as a dozen people were dragged into vans today, which means there are still people to be killed. There will always be people to kill.

"Untie me." Lila demanded of Blake. He shook his head. He didn't know if she was going to kill them or not.

"Melanie right." The twelve-year-old nodded. "If you don't untie me, we are all going to die including your brother." The girl looked back at her brother and stood still. Blake was definitely having a panic attack. Lila then added, "Blake, or whatever his name is, isn't in a stable position to keep any of you safe."

She would not move. They could all hear the guards coming. It was only a matter of time before they broke in and killed them all. A knock on the door made the full house go silent. No one dared to move.

"Open up." One guard roared. Melanie had thought over every ending of their situation. The only one where they made it out alive was if they trusted the stranger. Mel ran over to the girl, who had their fate in her hands.

"Mel... don't I can get us out of... this." Blake stuttered. He could hardly breathe, so Melanie untied Lila's other hand.

As soon as she had untied her hand, they heard the door get kicked down. Lila could tell the small boy was about to start crying, so she quickly placed a finger over his mouth. She whispered something to Noah, which automatically calmed him down.

She walked over to the bed and pulled a corner of the mattress, which revealed her survival bag and her food and water supply bag.

She stood next to the door frame.

"You three hide behind the other side of the bed" She passed a gun to Blake. "Only use it if I'm losing, but don't worry, I won't. You know how to use it right." Blake nodded. Lila felt sorry for the young boy, who couldn't be older than ten. He lives in a world where death, pain and torture are part of the daily cycle. She also felt sorry for Melanie and Blake. None of them knew what was about to happen.

Lila knew that the chances of getting out of there were less than twenty percent, but she had to figure away even if it meant she might not make it.

They could hear the guards storming into the house. It wouldn't be long till they found them.

Blake crawled, trying to not make a noise since the floor boards were always creaking. "Can you smell that" He asked. Lila didn't even notice it. The music was getting louder by the minute.

"Shit its gas! They're trying to kill us." Blake exclaimed. The kids were still hiding behind the bed.

"Kids come over here." Lila and Blake both passed them their jackets.

"Put it around your nose and mouth. And follow me." Lila whispered. They could hear plates being shattered and windows being smashed. She slowly opened the door, trying not to make a sound. Lila and Blake held their guns close. Lila glanced quickly down the stairs to see that there was only one guard. Luckily for her, the others were in the kitchen and her gun was silent. With swift movement and a thud, one of the Guards was dead. Lila quickly hurried them to Noah's room upstairs.

"We're going to have to jump down to the other house," Lila spoke in a calm tone.

Blake looked down at the other house. It wasn't the height that was the problem. The roof looked slippery and felt very unstable underneath her feet. It seemed they would either fall through it or off it.

Lila could tell Blake was debating whether to jump and die or stay and die. "Either way, it's a risk, but one way we are bound to die and the other way, not so much." Blake looked at her. He didn't want to agree with her, but he knew she was right.

"Alright". They didn't waste a moment they jumped. Mel and Noah gripped onto the roof of the building and slid down the other side. Lila and Blake both fell. The two kids rushed over to them. The rain was still lashing down so they could hardly see anything. Lila had fallen on top of Blake's chest. Lila tried to move herself. She looked down at him. He was unconscious but still breathing. Lila realized she was bleeding. She looked down to see that she had been shot. Lila was confident that she was strong enough to keep going.

"Pass me the jacket." Lila instructed swiftly. Noah handed her Blake's jacket back. Lila quickly wrapped it around Blake's head where it had bled. She stopped most of the bleeding. Gunshots were still blaring and they could still smell gas.

Melanie had put Lila's jacket on with her brother to keep him warm. Lila was wearing two jumpers. She tied one around her stomach to stop her own bleeding. She didn't tell the others. They were worried enough as it was. She looked to see where the bullet had come from, but it was hard to see in the heavy rain getting heavier. She saw a guard's uniform in the rain, so she shot at it. They all watched as their lifeless body hit the ground. Lila then looked back at Melanie, who was freezing. She was only wearing a thin top with leggings. Lila then took her jumper off and handed in to Melanie.

"We need to get going," Lila told them both.

"Don't leave him. Please don't leave him behind." Noah begged Lila.

"I wasn't planning on it. But you have to promise me if they catch up with us. You two need to leave us. Run into the forest and keep traveling north for a few hours. You will eventually come across a cabin. Go there..." Lila passed Melanie her survival bag.

"It will have all the stuff you need if I and Blake don't make it. Hopefully, it doesn't come to that." She whispers to Melanie. Lila didn't want Noah to worry even more that he already was.

Lila felt like she was going to pass out with the pain, but she tried her best to keep going for her and the others. She was hardly carrying Blake since he was nearly twice her height. Melanie and

Noah were only a few steps in front of her. The streets were covered in blood, but the rain was washing it away. In the morning, all the blues will think nothing of the murders that either happened in their streets or outside their walls.

Melanie kept looking back to see Lila struggling with Blake, so she turned back to help her. She wasn't much help, but it was enough to keep her walking.

Noah couldn't stop looking around. He felt something else was going to happen. He couldn't think of what could be worse, but he did not want to find out either.

Lila was grateful that Mel had helped her with Blake. She tried her best to hide it but she was also in pain. She didn't know how deep the bullet wound was, but she could feel the blood going down her leg.

Music had stopped, which was a good and a bad thing. The good thing was that no more purples would be killed unless they were on the street. The bad thing was, they were in the street.

"Quickly, it doesn't matter even if we have to drag him," Lila spoke rapidly. He was too heavy for them both to carry him while running, so they had to drag him. They stopped when they hit a fence surrounding an old house. Lila placed Blake against the fence. Noah was covering his ears, trying to block out the screams of innocent people.

Lila looked down the street. The teenager felt helpless. She couldn't do anything to help the people or put them out of their misery.

"Don't make a sound," Melanie whispered to them both.

Noah was holding back tears as they watched seven vans drive down the street. It felt as if the entire world went dark. An old man stepped out of one van. Lila watched as Melanie's and Noah's faces changed. They were already terrified, but now they looked petrified. Lila quickly undid her jumper and bound it again to stop the blood.

"Have you found them?" The man spoke coldly.

All the screams stopped, and the guards stood still. Lila wondered who this man was and why he could inflict such terror. She had never seen him before.

"Do I have to repeat myself?" He screamed.

One guard stepped forward. She was wearing a navy-blue bullet-proof suit. She had the blue mark on the front of the suit, which meant she was a leader of the group. The Guards were trained in groups of fifteen people and each group had a leader. Most leaders aren't scared of anything, but the women seemed terrified of this old man.

"SPEAK" he demanded.

"They ran." She mumbled.

The man looked furious. If looks could kill, she would have died that second.

"Two years I have told you to search for my grandson and his two followers and you have got nothing on them." The man bellowed.

Lila wondered who he was talking about. She hoped it had nothing to do with them. Melanie looked back at her brother, who looked as if he was struggling to breathe. She leaned into hug him but Noah just pushed her off him. He didn't know how to feel about the situation.

"All we know is that all three were accompanied by a girl. She looked around Blake's age. They couldn't have gone far. We shot the girl in the stomach."

Melanie looked at Lila and mouthed they shot you. Lila looked at her stomach again. She was still in unbearable pain but it looked like the bleeding had slowed down.

The old man looked at the women and shouted, "I gave you two years."

Melanie knew at that moment that he was going to kill the guard. Guards are obliged to follow the Gaol of honor handbook the number one rule is that it is against the king to kill a fellow guard. There had been very few cases of where that had actually happened but if you had a well known family name and enough power nobody cared.

The guard's corpse was dragged into a van. The van drove off, but nobody moved or showed emotion. They were emotionless uniforms controlled by the deadliest people on earth.

"My other grandson will control the search for the four runners." The man announced.

Theo stepped out of the van. The old man carried on speaking "As one of the king's most trusted men, I expect you to show my grandson respect."

Lila turned back around to face Melanie. The girl was shocked they were still being hunted still after two years. Melanie thought they would have given up by now, but she now knew they would hunt them to the ends of the earth. That wouldn't stop them from running.

"Melanie, do you remember what I told you to do?" she was about to interrupt her but Lila stopped her. Melanie nodded. "I will try to meet you there, but if they get me, I promise no matter what they do to me I will never tell them where you went."

Noah crawled over to Lila and Melanie. He hugged Lila in thanks then whispered the same thing that she had told him earlier, "If we go down then we go down together."

Lila looked at him, not knowing how to answer him, so she whispered, "But we're not going down, I promise." Melanie quickly grabbed Noah's hand and they disappeared into the forest. Lila didn't know if they were going down or not, but if they were, she knew she definitely wasn't alone and she wouldn't go down without a fight.

There was a piece of wood missing from the fence, so she stepped through it. It would give them both a bit more safety. She hastily pulled him through the fence.

Several times Lila checked to see if Blake was still breathing. He was, but he was out cold. He was covered in bruises and scratches.

Lila pulled one bag she was carrying closer to her. Melanie and Noah had taken the three bags she had handed them, which left her with three as well. One of them was filled with weapons and hunting tools. The second, filled with clothes and the third was a first aid kit.

She removed her jacket from his head and grabbed the flask she had in her bag. It had alcohol in it which would help clean his wound. It didn't need stitches. Lucky him, she thought. She definitely did. She tied a bandage around his head.

Lila only had enough for one dose of painkillers, so she kept it for Blake when he woke up. She then cleaned her bullet wound. She was still in pain, but it felt better. She could hardly keep her eyes open. She knew she shouldn't, but she ended up drifting off to sleep.

In the morning she woke up abruptly to the sound of people talking and laughing in the street. She could see a few guards stationed at the end of either side of the street. Luckily for them, they were still safely out of sight.

Lila looked down at her stomach. Thankfully, the stitches had stopped the bleeding. Blake was still out, but she crawled over to him.

"Blake please wake up I can't carry you again" she begged him. Lila planned for them both to leave as soon as it got dark. She fell back asleep, since she was still exhausted.

Chapter 6

On the Run

"Wake up" A voice said to Lila. To her surprise it was Blake he was awake. He then added "How did we get here."

She quickly cut him off "We have to go now. We have to get to Noah and Melanie."

"You left them" Blake accused her.

"Not exactly. I told them where to go to and it's not like I could leave you to defend your lifeless body. Plus, you can lecture me on the way there."

As the wind blew, the trees hung tall like a city, the breeze pushing through the mass of leaves, dark branches reaching for the warmth of the sun that they will never reach. Lila didn't need a compass or a map. She could get to her cabin with her eyes closed. Blake was still furious and going on about how she shouldn't have left the kids on their own.

"Here" She passed him the painkillers and he gladly took them but he was still mad. Lila was still in pain and it got worse with every breath and step she took.

Slowly, the sun was escaping its void of darkness but in less than twenty-four hours it would return to its land of emptiness.

They walked in silence until the cabin was in sight. Blake started sprinting towards the cabin he needed to know if they were okay as he reached the door Melanie and Noah walked out.

"You're both okay" He shouted in relief.

"We thought you would both be dead" Noah whispered.

"How is she?" Melanie asked Blake as she watched Lila become visible.

Blake turned around. Melanie quickly ran in the cabin to try find the pain killers. Blake ran back up to Lila and shouted "Why didn't you tell me you were shot."

Blake was annoyed that she didn't tell him but he also felt guilty. Guilty because he screamed at her for leaving the kids when she would've only slowed them down.

Instead of shouting again he just said "I'm sorry" they both slowly walked back to the house Melanie handed Lila a cup of water and a painkiller.

"I'm going to get some sleep if that's alright." Lila said.

"Hope you feel better" Melanie spoke as Lila left the room.

Blake sat down on one of the chairs, Melanie then explained what had happened. How Lila had to carry him and how she helped. Then Noah went on about how Blake's family are still hunting them down.

Blake slept on the couch whereas Melanie and Noah slept in the spare room. His overactive mind kept him awake most nights

Every time Blake closed his eyes he would wake back up in 'the gaol'. He would see his cell mate Isabella. They were always arguing or fighting about something. They hated each other. The only thing Blake ever regrets is leaving her in 'the Gaol' instead of saving her.

The truth is Blake didn't have a choice but to leave her there. Isabella was being tortured the day he left. Greyson had passed the wards and helped him escape.

Lila slowly opened the door. "Are you okay, you seem off?" Lila whispered as she walked through the door.

"I'm fine." Blake lied.

Lila walked over and sat next to him. Eventually Blake drifted off to off to sleep which left Lila to her thoughts.

She didn't know how to feel she had almost been killed twice over the past forty- eight hours.

PART 2
ONLY
TIME WILL
TELL

CHAPTER 7

DEATH IS INEVITABLE

THREE HOURS EARLIER

Jordan Amulet; a girl who was hardly noticeable. She was always there. Whether she was lurking behind corners or blending in with the crowd. She knew more about other people than she did herself.

Jordan had been alone for most of her life. It feels a lifetime ago that she had her family. Her family was small, despite that they were known for their secrets.

Like most purple children her family were killed. Her story was different. Unusually, Jordan was allowed to live. An old guard who had spent his full life being turned into an emotionless solider took pity on a thirteen-year-old child.

Four years later and not much had changed about her life. She decided to go off the map. No one knows a thing about her but she knows a lot more than she should. If 'The gaol' ever figured out how much she knew they would take her dead or alive.

It had to have been around eleven o'clock at night. It was pitch black outside and the stars shone bright. The moon and the stars are the only light source that the street has when it gets dark. All the street lamps are smashed and broken. The cobbled stones are crooked and chipped. Jordan always felt like this part of the city was stuck in the 18th century whereas the rest of the world had moved on.

Jordan decided to stay out of sight tonight. She always felt like someone was watching over her, whether it was her parents or whoever's out there.

About six months ago, some of the purples arranged a raid to show them that they're still here and they are not going anywhere. They got all sorts of things from stores, warehouses and even farms. For once 'The gaol' were on the losing side. But everything must come to a conclusion at one point. Jordan decided to stay inside for that month even though she had barely enough food to survive it was still safer. There was only one place that wasn't destroyed or completely raided.

The shop was quite far away from the shelter Jordan lives in. It's technically not a shop since no one really owns it but it has few boxes of supplies. It was quite abandoned to be honest but it was still worth the travel.

Jordan could finally see the shop in sight but she could feel something was off. She reached for her pocket to check if she brought anything she could use to protect herself with. The one day I don't bring my pocket knife, she scolded herself silently

Music started blasting through the only things that weren't broken in this street. The speakers.

Shit that's not music she thought to herself. Jordan wanted to run but she felt herself glued to the floor. Even though growing up like every normal purple she had never been in a situation where her life was actually threatened. Yes, she knew what to do it was just if she could do it. Would I be able to kill someone she thought to herself? Even though she could hear screaming, tyres dragging along the cobbled road and even the blood hitting the walls her feet stayed glued to the floor.

Jordan couldn't move she wasn't in plain sight but she didn't know if they could see her or not. She couldn't see them but the pictures in her mind were frightening enough.

It was as if her mind had become clear, she knew what she had to do. Run.

Quickly, she ran down the street. As she thought she was nearly safe she tripped over an even cobbled stone. Blood was dripping down her head. The gunshots had got louder the screaming had become nearer and the endless marching became quicker.

She knew she was going to die. That was the one thing Jordan was never scared of. Her mother always told her 'Why fear something that's inevitable. Even though she wasn't scared she didn't want to die not yet anyway an especially not like this.

Then everything went black.

Chapter 8

Great! Another person to save.

Jason Jonz a teenage boy who was often referred to as the invisible man. He had escaped death more times than he can count. 'The gaol' know not a thing about Jason. He's one of the few people that the king wants personally executed. He never stays in one place longer than two months.

When he was younger his eyes were a bright grey colour but now, they've turned more of a sterling grey colour. Growing up he always felt like an outsider. The day his mark appeared he had to make it look like he was dead.

He would never forget their cries when the head guard told them about my death. Jason has to remind himself every day that he had no choice they were cold blooded deadly killers. Who would have killed him the second they knew?

It was colder than usual Jason thought to himself he knew what was going to happen. Hours before hand he tried to get people out and to leave quickly before they were killed. This street was not packed with purples but there's never usually this many of them in one place. The boy knocked on every door and window to warn people. Few people took notice of him since it had been over three years since the last death night happened.

Death night the night where they are hunted and most are killed. There was never a pattern to the death nights but after a year most people thought they'd decided to stop the mass killings. But Jason knew they hadn't. Unlike most people he still has his parents but his story is different to others. His farther is a purple whereas his mother is a blue. His mother Sky protected her husband she kept their secret until   Jason turned sixteen, he found out his mother was planning against his family so he left.

For some reason he knew there was going to be another 'Death night' he had no idea why he felt like this was going to happen. He wasn't one hundred percent sure if he was right or wrong but he wasn't willing to take the risk of him being right.

Jason was standing on top of a half-collapsed building. He looked down at the full city it was quiet too quiet Jason thought. He knew the screaming would come he just hoped people would take his warning and leave.

The rain was getting heavier and heavier. Jason stood drenched looking down at the ground. That's when it began the deadliest sound blasted through speakers.

The screams began he leaned back against a wall and he tried to block the sound out. He watched as people were slaughtered in the street. The one thing Jason feared in this world was being unable to save everyone.

He felt helpless in this situation he watched as people fled for their life.

The stairs were creaky and some of the steps were broken. Slowly he pushed the broken door open. Jason quickly glanced down the street to check if it was safe to leave.

The road was stained with blood and vans were pulling up in the alley. He hid behind an old rubbish bin. The rain was getting heavier and the screaming was getting louder.

Jason could hear the pain in their screams. He watched helplessly as children no older than nine were dragged into the vans. They were screaming and kicking at the guards but they had no chance. Jason thought to himself he had to risk it.

He stood up abruptly. He shot at the two guards. Jason listened as their two lifeless bodies hit the ground. Without a moment to think he grabbed the children from the van and ran.

They ran towards a dead end. The two kids were out of breath and could hardly stand up.

"Why did you do that?" One of the small children questioned him. Jason had no words the two children knew that most people would have kept running and left while they still had a chance.

"Hide here until morning" Jason spoke quietly. One the children mouthed the words thank you while Jason sprinted down the alley. The music kept getting louder and louder whereas the rain was getting heavier.

He couldn't tell if the gunshots were getting closer or further away people were dying everywhere. He checked every body he found none were alive but he still had hope that one of them were still breathing. There were three guards standing around a girl who looked dead but Jason couldn't tell.

The vans were driving away only to return minutes later. Each time they were filled with more innocent people. He couldn't help but feel guilty about them.

Jason only ever wore black clothes which helped him blend into the shadows so no one would ever see him at first glance.

"I need backup six street way we have a runner" A women's voice said over the radio.

"Sir?" One of the guards questioned. It was at this moment he realised this was the perfect distraction for him.

"I have a bit of a sore throat today." The women spoke while trying to disguise her voice as a man's. Jason chuckled he wasn't laughing at how bad the women was lying. He was laughing at how they had believed her.

Surprisingly, they left the girl in the street. Jason stood over her for some reason he felt like she was still alive.

Then he heard it. The sound had stopped. He couldn't think he hastily scooped the girl up and sprinted toward an empty shop. Quickly, Jason placed her behind an old rotted desk. It wouldn't be long before the street was filled with guards.

Then he heard it, the back door had opened. Without thinking Jason hid himself underneath the desk. The stranger looked as if she was only a lifeless body but he could hear breathing which meant there was still hope for her he thought to himself.

Funny thing they live in a world where hope is a rare thing few purples still believe in hope. Most people believe that hope is pointless but Jason always believes that if you can find hope you can eventually find peace. But everyone even Jason knew that peace was a long way off. He could see a girl.

Chapter 9

Fifty-fifty is a good ratio

Jason stayed out of sight the stranger who laid next to him was still unconscious. The other girl was kneeling behind another broken door everything in this place was broken.

The girl had almond coloured skin with dark brown curly hair that flowed to the end of her back. The street filled with the deadliest guards. Jason was debating whether this was worth it whereas the other girl in the shop realised she wasn't alone.

The girl stayed silent she couldn't risk it. Since they are hiding, they might not kill her she thought silently. The rain poured through the broken tiles giving the deserted shop no protection. The only noise that could be heard was the lashing sound of the rain hitting the wooden floor.

They were completely powerless compared to the guards. They were outnumbered at least one hundred times.

"What." The stranger under the desk said while trying to catch her breath. Jason quickly covered her mouth to not startle the other stranger who was in there with them. Who are you Jason mouthed to the girl who was sitting next to him?

"Jordan Amulet. Who are you?" Jordan questioned him. He was full of questions the main one was why was she unconscious.

"Jason Jonz." He spoke quietly. The girl crawled towards the desk and pulled the dusty sheet off the desk. Jordan ran across to the other side of the room she was going to be sick. The stranger ran over too while trying to stay out of sight. She held Jordan's hair out of the way.

"Are you okay" Jason spoke with a quivering tone. The stranger glared at him which made him go silent. Finally, the street was empty they could leave but they both stayed Jason and the girl both knew if they left her, she would most likely die.

"I'm fine" Jordan's voice was no more than a whisper. She then spoke "If you don't mind me asking who you are?"

The stranger sat next to the exhausted girl and Jason moved over to them.

"Brooklyn Scott and who are you?" She asked calmly.

"That's Jordan Amulet" He said while pointing at Jordan "And I'm Jason Jonz."

They sat in silence for a while they were all exhausted but Jordan felt like she was at deaths door. Blood was dripping out of the corner of Jordan's mouth. She felt like she was chocking and she couldn't breathe. Jason quickly noticed and grabbed for his bag that was almost empty. He passed his flask to her she spat the water straight out.

"I'm fine. I'm fine" She repeated. Brooklyn looked at Jason they both knew she was nowhere near fine. They both had the same worried look on their face.

"No, you idiot! Blood isn't supposed to spill out of your mouth" He blurted out.

"You don't look like you're okay…." Brooklyn spoke calmly. Jordan hardly knew these people and they were worried about her. Nobody had ever worried about before and she didn't like the feeling. The feeling of upsetting the people who oddly care about you.

"Just leave me I can't walk." Jordan spoke bluntly. They both looked shocked if they were going to leave her, they would've left by now.

Jason stood up and walked up to her and picked her up bridal style.

"Problem solved" Jason said while Jordan was rolling her eyes. Deep down she was grateful that they were saving her but she wasn't one to show emotions.

"We don't know if there still out there it's a fifty-fifty chance we will make it out of here alive." Brooklyn exclaimed.

Jason looked at her and said "Good thing I like those odds."

They were used to the feeling risking it all. Without thinking they ran they weren't running to anywhere in particular. Jordan could barely keep her eyes open with each breath she took her eye lids got heavier and heavier. Brooklyn was running ahead of them "Do you have a plan" Brooklyn shouts back at Jason.

Jason shook his head no and answered with "Plans are for the weak." Brooklyn interrupted with "Also for the smart."

It's funny friendship it can come in mysterious ways.

"I have an idea where we can go to." Brooklyn said as she stopped running. They didn't stop to think about it Jason just followed Brooklyn. They finally stopped running when they came across a block of flats. Jason stood in the middle of the road still carrying Jordan as Brooklyn walked up to a door.

"Brooklyn what are you doing?" Jason spoke quietly. He started to walk over to her as Brooklyn opened the door. It was pitch black inside the flat and the windows were boarded up it didn't look like anyone lived in there.

"Follow me" Brooklyn said in a hushed tone. Jason followed her into one of the rooms and placed the unconscious girl on the bed. They both went back into the other room and sat silently. They didn't know what to talk about.

"Do you think she's going to make it" Jason asked casually. Brooklyn looked over to him unsure what to say.

"I'm going to go check on her" Brooklyn spoke quietly while she left the room.

All of a sudden there was screaming in the other room without thinking Jason picked up an old broken lamp. As he walked through the door the screaming stopped but Brooklyn started shouting at him "What is wrong with you?"

Jason looked deadly confused. "What's wrong with me why the hell was she screaming" Jason blurted out. Jordan had started to calm down.

"She thought they had caught her but I have reassured her that they haven't" Brooklyn spoke while giving Jason a death stare.

"How do you know each other" Brooklyn asked them.

Jason looked at Jordan and answered with "We've known each other since we were five." Jason leaned in to hug her but she shoved him off straight away. Jason then thought to himself she's easy to annoy.

"I'm Jordan and this is the person I met yesterday." Jordan spoke confidentially.

Slowly, Jason walked backwards out the room. Jason then thought to himself that he may have overacted but he wasn't going to tell them that.

Chapter 10
Most ridiculous way to die

"Was he like this yesterday" Brooklyn chuckled. Jordan thought to herself she had known him for less than two days and she has no words to explain him.

"He's crazy." Jordan laughed. She then added "How long do you think I will be unable to run for." Brooklyn stopped laughing she knew the dangers of not being able to run, she had been in a similar position less than three months ago. The only difference was Brooklyn was alone and she promised herself that if she ever found someone who couldn't save themselves, she would try her best to help them. Plus, Brooklyn could tell from the beginning that they would end up being friends.

"Around a month or two but you can stay here for as long as you want." Brooklyn spoke with sympathy.

"I wouldn't want to be a burden." Jordan mumbled.

"You wouldn't be a burden. It would be quite fun actually." Brooklyn answers. She then thought to herself it would be fun to do one normal thing in this lifetime because being hunted to the ends of the earth isn't exactly what I would call normal.

"Would about Jason?" Brooklyn spoke.

Jordan glanced back at the door she could tell Jason was sitting behind it because the door kept slowly opening and shutting

"I bet you he's already decided he is moving in." Jordan spoke as she pointed at the door.

Jason pranced in while saying "Yes I am and you owe me one. Plus, it's not like I have anywhere important to be."

"How do we owe you again"? Brooklyn says confidently. You would have thought Brooklyn had killed someone the way Jason reacted to this.

"You owe me because if it wasn't for me you would have got caught" He then turned around to face Jordan

"And you would have died by, what was it oh yeah tripping over a rock." They all burst out laughing, so much that Jordan's stiches were hurting.

Chapter 11

Who is Brooklyn Scott?

"I guess we owe you a lot then but we can't stay here." Living alone is safe but what's a life without freedom and fun. Jordan and Brooklyn seem to be getting along well.

"I have another house." Brooklyn said excitedly.

"Let's get going before it gets dark" Jason says without a minute to lose.

I have lived in this part of town for years Jordan thought to herself but maybe a change of scenery will be a good thing.

"There's a small minor issue" Brooklyn interrupts Jordan's thoughts with what can only be bad news. It can't be that bad Jason thought to himself.

"It's not far from the king's palace." On the outside of the wall that surrounds the main buildings there are a few houses but they are heavily guarded. Going anywhere near the wall classes as a suicide mission.

"We can't go there. Do you want to die?" Jordan says bluntly.

"Why don't we take a vote?" Jason suggests.

"Does democracy even still exist?" Jordan says to Jason.

"Okay so we're taking a vote all those in favour of staying raise your hand." Brooklyn was trying so hard to keep a straight face but she was failing miserably,

Jordan was the only one that raised her hands. Sadly, that meant that we had to go to the place where I have been running from my entire life. The direct centre of the world also known as the king's city Jordan thought to herself. The guard is exactly twenty miles away from the king's city.

"We should leave tomorrow morning." Jason spoke quietly. The others both shook their heads in agreement. Jordan didn't like the idea of it not one bit it felt as if she was getting closer and closer to her downfall.

The next morning, they all woke up at the crack of dawn. When Jordan first arrived in this street, she could never have imagined leaving. Honestly, she didn't even think she would live to see her 17th birthday. As there crossing through the city there was a big commotion but they managed to avoid all contact with any of the king's uniforms. They were right, the whole world ignored last night and carried on. The rain had also washed all the blood off the roads.

"Just down this street" Brooklyn was directing them down this. Extravagant Street. Jason had never seen anything like this in his whole nineteen years of living. The apartments were all connected it was if they were going to be hidden in plain sight. Brooklyn was right nobody would suspect them. Jason looked like he was in heaven, even Brooklyn was filled with excitement.

"Shall we go inside" Jason whispered. Brooklyn grabbed the keys from inside her back pack.

"Woah you didn't tell us this was your place!" Jason was practically screaming with enjoyment. He wasn't wrong though she never told them her apartment was this spectacular.

"It was my mother's apartment. I'm going to the market to get some supplies if anyone wants to come" Brooklyn asked them both.

"Can I come" Jason said to Brooklyn. She nodded and Jordan walked up the stairs and went back to sleep she was still in unbearable pain.

As they were walking, they could see the streets were packed with deadly uniforms.

The screams were getting louder people were dying in the middle of the streets and others were being carried into black bullet-proof vans but everyone else around them just carried on walking they weren't thinking anything about it. The two looked at each other in terror. They both should have left straight away but it felt as if they were both stuck to the ground and unable to move. An armed solider walked in front of them. The first time in my life I was terrified of being caught Jason thought to himself for the first time in years I had people in my life who I cared about.

"Show me your wrist" He spoke as if he knew, that's what terrified them most. Jason glanced back at Brooklyn who was as shocked as he was but then she mouthed one word he will never forget, "RUN".

Without thinking he did what she said and he ran through the alley he didn't know if they were following him or where Brooklyn was but he knew one thing was that neither of them were in sight which was more worrying, but he didn't stop running he kept thinking at least one of us has to get back to Jordan. His mind focused on getting through the door, he wanted to get there before his mind allowed him to drown with guilt.

"Jason you gave me a heart attack." Jordan shouted down the stairs.

"Brooklyn … we ran into she told me to run." The room started closing in on me. Jason felt like he wasn't in the same room anymore he didn't feel safe to be honest he couldn't feel anything. He blacked out.

"He must've passed out Jordan thought to herself". Jordan couldn't help but wonder what had happened, she stayed with him for a few hours but she must've fell asleep. Three hours later Jason woke up panicking Jordan ran straight up to him.

"Shush it's okay you're okay go back to sleep we can deal with the situation tomorrow" He finally drifted off to sleep, but Jordan stayed awake just in case he woke up or Brooklyn came back from wherever she was. Jordan kept imagining the worst which would be finding out that Brooklyn was killed or worse tortured. She could hear Jason get up from upstairs it must have been about 6 in the morning but for some reason she wasn't up. Jason looked as if he had seen a ghost.

"Jason what happened yesterday." She asked him as he slowly sat down beside her. He looked at her but he couldn't bring himself to say anything.

"We were walking to the market and there were more guards than usual. They were killing people in the streets. Then one of them approached us and I didn't know what to do but Brooklyn told me to run so I did. I know I should have stayed with her."

Jordan wanted the world to stay still. She couldn't chase the problems anymore every time she began to do something the world would shift again.

"We will get her back." Were the only words Jordan could get out? Everything was confusing Jordan couldn't put a word to her problems the only thing that was clear to her was that they had to leave.

"How, how do we get her back there's a chance she's already dead." Jason spoke in an angered tone. Jordan looked at him she could tell this was breaking him, but how can you break something that's already broken.

She shrugged her shoulders she had no words there was a chance that the girl had already been killed but she refused to believe that.

"Do you remember where you ran from?" He nodded "We better get going then."

The full way to the main market they walked in silence but everyone around them was unusually quiet.

"I don't think we should have come." Jason looked confused but this was a classic come back to the crime scene. They were waiting for him, without thinking

Jordan quickly grabbed Jason's arm and took him through a street neither of them had ever seen before.

"Stay quiet and stay behind me no matter what." She says in a hushed tone. Within seconds a guard came from nowhere.

"Two of you" He pauses. "I am only supposed to bring the boy." He says with a murderous voice. He reaches for his gun unaware of who he is about to point it at. Without a warning Jordan jumped in front of Jason and shoots him dead.

"Are you okay" he says to her.

Did he not hear me Jordan thought to herself?

"I told you to stay behind me." Jason knew she was angry with that response.

"It's not like he was going to kill me." He shouted at her.

"But he could've and what would have happened then we would both be dead." She screams back at him.

"We're both going to be killed at one point or another you've been living this life what 19 years. You think you would have learned that nobody lives a long happy life." Jason screams at her again. Jordan's whole existence was a lie nobody even knew she existed till a day ago.

"You're right." She whispers.

"Have you got the boy." voice says over a two-way radio. Jordan looked towards Jason who mouths the words be quiet and get ready to run.

"Hey, how are you?" He says sarcastically to the walkie-talkie. Does he have a death wish Jordan thought? There was mumbling on the other side of the line but nobody could make out what they were saying.

He then adds "Oh, we killed your guy whoever he was just so you know it's going to be a lot harder to catch us than getting one of your weakling's. Your majesty. Love from the invisible man!" Yeah, he has a death wish Jordan thought to herself. Quickly Jason grabs her hand again and they start running no clue where there running to. They get to the end of the alley and without thinking they take another right turn; they could turn back and chance it but they didn't want to risk it. They finally stop when they reached the end of the city centre.

"Where are we going" Jordan asked.

"I don't know but we have to leave the main city and we can't go back to the house." Nowhere to go, but they keep running. Getting caught is no option neither is not finding Brooklyn.

Chapter 12

For now

They didn't stop running not until they hit the end of this deadly city.

"Where are we going" Jordan repeated. There was literally nowhere to run to.

"I don't know we need to find somewhere anywhere, I guess where staying out here." Jason spoke while pointing at the frost covered forest. Jordan had always hated the outdoors; when she was a child, she would hardly ever leave her room. Then again, they both must adapt to the situation, even the worst thing imaginable can be normalized.

"If we keep going south, we will hit a place no one would dare to venture." Jason whispered to Jordan.

"Seriously you don't need to whisper no one has followed us we're safe." Jordan stated.

"For now." Jason added to her positive sentence. The forest. Few people would ever venture this far south. If they weren't killed by the blue's they would most likely be eaten by the wolves. This was all wolf territory hey are vicious.

Jordan laid back against one of the trees.

"We better take it in turns sleeping but only if you trust me." Jason mumbled

"Of course, I trust you if I didn't, I definitely would not have let you move in with us plus who else a I meant trust it's not like I know anyone other than you and Brooklyn" She explained.

"Do you ever think life would be much better as a seeker?" Jason inquired. Without a doubt Jason would change his mark it was an easier life, but an easier life doesn't always mean a good life

"Yes, life would be easier." Jason felt as if she was reading his mind but he knew she was going to add something to her statement.

"But having to kill innocent people who have done nothing but live their lives, I know I couldn't" Jason understood where she was coming from but he would always choose to change.

"I will take the first watch." Jason spoke. She nodded and fell straight to sleep. His eyes felt like they were getting heavier he didn't realise it but he must've drifted off to sleep.

PART 3
Death

Will

Succeed

Chapter 13

Back to the Cabin

Survive the day

Noah was outside with Blake. Blake started to trust Lila a bit more but she still felt like he was cautious around them. They kept her in the dark about the Hunter's and Lila's mother but Lila knew they would eventually tell her plus she didn't want to pry. They all had their life stories to tell but most of them were secrets not stories and secrets can either bring people closer together or push them apart. Melanie spent all her time in her room a few times Blake went to check on her and he could tell she had been crying but Blake didn't know what to do or say. He could get no words out no words could ever make her feel safe. Noah seemed to be happier but he hardly ever spoke. Blake couldn't help but feel like something terrible is going to happen.

"How are you today?" Blake spoke while walking into the kitchen. Lila was shocked he hardly ever spoke to her but she just answered with "I'm fine, are you?" He nodded and walked back out.

Surprisingly, Melanie walked in and sat down at the table. Lila could tell the girl had been crying her eyes were a glossy pink colour.

"Do you need a hand?" Melanie mumbled.

"Are you sure? Can you clean the dishes". Melanie walked over and started cleaning. For some reason Melanie had always found cleaning relaxing.

"What's going to happen to us?" Melanie asked Lila quietly. Lila looked at her she wanted to tell the girl she was going to be fine and everything would be alright but even she knew that wasn't true.

"I don't know Mel. But I know we're fine for now" She says in a calming tone.

"Yeah, I guess" Melanie said. Melanie didn't trust many people but for some reason she felt safer around Lila.

"We're back." Noah shouts with excitement from the living room. He runs into the kitchen filled with joy.

"Hey, Mel and Lila." He spoke excitedly. I've never seen him this happy before, even Blake looked happy for once, sometimes I forget that he has emotions Melanie thought to herself.

"We ran round the forest and climbed the trees" Noah explains with joy.

"We had a good time. Didn't we buddy?" Blake says to Noah. Noah nods.

"Mel can you set the table." Lila asked her she quickly went over to the table.

 Lila and Blake walk in with the food. It smells like heaven Blake thought.

After dinner Melanie and Noah ran straight to their room. Melanie stayed awake for a while she couldn't help but wonder what was going to happen to them but she blocked it out and fell into a deep sleep.

Chapter 14
Nothing is Permanent

It had been over a week since the incident, Melanie looked happier but anyone with eyes could tell that she was still terrified. Blake couldn't get around the fact that Theo was still hunting them.

It had to have been around three in the morning but Lila couldn't sleep her mind was too preoccupied with how they were going to survive this nightmare when the odds are stacked against them. She walked sleepily into the living room to her surprise she wasn't the only one whose mind was keeping them awake.

"I couldn't sleep. What about you?" Lila spoke quietly.

"Noah kicked me in his sleep." Melanie muttered.

"Well, I was planning on going on a walk if you want to come with me." She asks me.

"That sounds amazing" I say. The forest was like a winter wonderland during the day but at night it felt like a fairy tale. The windows of the cabin were glazed with a layer of frost the clouds were so low it was as if you could touch them.

They both walked in silence they didn't need words just knowing that they were with someone they trusted was enough. Lila's long curly hair was covered in snowflakes it was freezing but peaceful. After a while they both decided to go back to the cabin. They both really wished they hadn't. Like all fairy tales this one had to come to an end.

Lila could tell something was wrong even before she opened the door it was as if all the darkness in the world was trapped behind this one door. Without hesitating Melanie opened the door the sun had already started rising. Blake grabbed them both, closed the door, and locked it. Noah stood in the corner of the room he looked devastated. Melanie rushed over to him she tried her best to comfort him but even she didn't know what had happened this time.

"What's happening?" Lila screams but Blake couldn't get any words out. It wasn't until Lila looked at them both to realise that they were both drenched in blood.

"They've sent people after us. There were these two people near to the cabin. They were talking about killing purples. We panicked so we knocked them out." Blake explained. Lila was horrified. What I don't get is why they would bring them back to the cabin Melanie thought to herself.

"What colour." Lila asked calmly. I think we all knew the answer to that question though Melanie thought to herself.

"Purple. It could be a fake though." Noah says quietly. I guess I was wrong then Melanie thought.

Lila was furious again there was a high chance that they were innocent.

"You kidnaped them." Lila shouts at Blake. Melanie looked shocked but she took her brother into another room to try get the blood out of his clothes.

"No, they could have still been sent here to kill us" Alec shouts back.

"They could've been talking about the topic. Not everyone is sent to kill us." Lila screams back at him.

"It would make sense though wouldn't it I'm wanted in every bloody country and so are the kids. I hardly know anything about you but I bet you're wanted as well." Blake yelled at her.

He was right. She hated the feeling of being wrong even about the most ridiculous things but for once she understood where he was coming from.

Melanie on the other hand was trying to get the blood off Noah's clothes she was fuming with Blake for putting her brother in this position. The screaming from the basement was getting louder, it almost could've come out of a horror film. Without thinking she walked out of the bathroom and headed towards the basement door.

The door creaked open and the room fell silent the screaming stopped they must've heard the door. The only sound that could be heard was Lila and Blake arguing in the other room. Without thinking Melanie closed the door behind her. She was curious to who was down there. Then again curiosity is what killed the cat Melanie thought to herself. The stairs felt like if she took one wrong step she would fall straight through. Melanie began to feel the wall for some sort of light switch. Eventually she found one and the lights flickered. There was a girl lying across the floor her face was covered in bruises and her head was bleeding she had to have been around Blake and Lila's age. A boy who was also about Blake's age was passed out next to her he was also covered in cuts and bruises.

The stranger looked up at Melanie she looked terrified, but it took her a few moments to realise it wasn't her the stranger feared. Melanie spun around to see her younger brother standing at the top of the crooked stairs.

"Please help us" The stranger begged Melanie and Noah.

Within seconds they could hear Lila and Blake running to the basement.

"Noah Mel are you okay." Blake spoke while standing in front of them.

"I promise we are not here to hurt you" The girl spoke, they could still hear the fear in her voice no matter how hard she tried to hide it.

CHAPTER 15

STRANGERS

They are going to kill me the girl thought to herself.

"We aren't going to hurt you." Lila spoke in a calming tone, but the stranger didn't believe her. "Any more than Blake already has. I' m Lila, this is Blake, Melanie and Noah." Lila said.

"I'm Jordan and this idiot is Jason." Jordan explained. Melanie smiled at her there was a small chance they were sent here to kill them, but it didn't feel that way at all. Quickly, Melanie untied them both, Blake was starting to doubt himself they weren't sent here he silently thought.

He knelt next to them both "I won't hurt either of you unless you give us a reason." He says in a threatening tone.

I don't know if that was supposed to be reassuring or not but I at least no they aren't going to kill us, right now at least Jordan thought to herself.

Jordan watched as Blake carried Jason up the stairs the girl didn't feel safe at all.

Lila helped Jordan to her feet Jordan was still in pain from the shop, but she didn't let them know that. If they know I am injured, they know I have a weakness Jordan thought to herself while climbing the stairs that felt endless.

Lila sat Jordan down in the living room and then Lila left. The girl couldn't help but think where Jason was, she didn't like that they were keeping them apart.

Lila walked back in the room with two cups of steaming hot coffee. Jordan had always hated coffee, but she stayed silent anyways.

"The kids have gone outside but I can still see them." Blake informs Lila. They all look out the window to see Noah and Melanie having the time of their lives, but they all knew that wouldn't last long.

"How is coffee an essential" Alec says sarcastically.

"Alec I practically live off coffee." Lila answered.

The snow had finally stopped but they could still feel the coldness in the air. It's always cold in this part of the city.

"How old are you, Jordan?" Blake says while changing the subject.

"I'm 17 nearly 18" Jordan says quietly.

"I'm literally surrounded by children." He says trying to annoy them both.

"Actually, you're not Jason is nineteen." Jordan spoke bluntly. Blake walked back out the room. Jordan adds "Is he always like this?"

"I've known him for a week and from what I can tell it's like having another child. How long have you known Jason?" Lila asked Jordan.

"Too long" Jordan paused. "Nearly one week." Lila burst out laughing.

"Is he that bad?" She asked. He's not bad he's just highly annoying Jordan thought to herself

"Let's just say when I was going to move in with a girl called Brooklyn. He burst through the door and said he was moving in too." Jordan paused again. "I had known him less than 24 hours when he said that." Lila started laughing again.

"How did you meet him?" She asks me.

Jordan explained the situation they were in and how they must find Brooklyn as soon as possible. Jordan knew that she shouldn't trust them, but she couldn't help but talk about what had happened. Her mind was focusing on surviving while her heart was focused on finding Brooklyn.

"I met Alec and the kids that same night." Jordan explained how she met Melanie and Noah and how Alec doesn't trust her, but that's understandable giving their situation

CHAPTER 16

A Feeling Worse than Hell

Jason woke up to an uncomfortable feeling he was surrounded with deafening thoughts.

I haven't lost both have I he thought to himself. He couldn't help but think the worst of this situation. Without thinking he ran over to the half-bordered window. The wood was only covering half of the window nails were pointing out. He looked out to see the man that had beaten him half to death he was with two younger children why am I still here Jason panicked.

Without thinking anything through he ran through the cabin he had no clue what he was going to say.

"Jason your awake!" A surprised voice said coming from behind him. He turned around he had no clue who this small girl was he just looked at her with a confused face.

"Where's Jordan." Jason demanded. The girl motioned him to follow her he did, but he kept his guard up.

As soon as he saw her, he ran up to her and hugged her while saying, "I couldn't find you. Who are these people and what do they want with us?". Jason followed Jordan back to the room he was trapped in. To his surprise she hugged him. It was as if Jordan was saying they're safe... For a moment only a moment they both forgot all their worries it was as if they were ignoring the world even if it was only for a few minutes.

Jordan broke the peaceful silence with "How do we get Brooklyn back now?" What am I meant to say I would do anything to take her place in hell but there is no number of words that can change the fact, that I have no clue where she is or if she's even alive, Jason thought to himself? Instead of burdening her with every nightmare he was thinking of Jason whispered, "I don't know but we will find a way to get her back."

Jason looked at the door to see the people who had taken them but he noticed that Jordan wasn't bothered by the fact that they had come in, but he wasn't calm at all.

"We're not going to hurt you." Lila reminded them.

"This is Lila, Blake, Melanie and Noah." They seemed like genuinely nice people even though they kidnapped us and tried to kill me but I'm not one to hold a grudge against anyone other than if they deserved it Jason thought in silence.

For the rest of Night Jason and Jordan thought of countless plans of how to get Brooklyn back but they all resulted in their deaths.

Chapter 17

Light at the End of the Tunnel

Lila fell asleep quite quickly it had been an exhausting day for all of them, but she was not ready for what she was waking up to. Lila was woken up abruptly to the uncomforting sounds of crying and yelling. It was as if it was instinct without thinking too much into what could happen, she grabbed her knives and bolted into the living room. Jordan was trying to comfort Noah and Melanie, while Blake started turning all the blinds which made the room pitch black.

"What's happening?" Lila demanded.

"They're coming" Jason says. Two words just those two words can change every one's mood in the house. Those two words are the definition of life and death.

Even Noah was panicking, Blake was rushing everyone Melanie didn't say a word.

"How long have we got" Jordan says calmly. They all looked unsure until Blake answered with "Less than five minutes." I could hear gunshots and screams in the distance. How did they find us, I have lived here for years I guess I didn't realize I wasn't the only one who lived here Lila thought?

Noah looked out the window his heart sank he watched as two black vans drove recklessly through the forest, but they stopped less than two minutes away from the cabin.

Blake pulled him away from the window he was about to start yelling but there was no time to.

"Guys we have to go." Noah spoke in a voiceless tone. It was as if it was instinct everyone knew what to do. Lila took a quick glance at the half-covered window the Guards were getting closer by the second.

"Where's the quickest way out" Blake spoke quietly to try not to draw any more attention to the cabin.

"And how is this going to get us out of here" Jason says angrily. Jordan nudges him as if to say calm down. Within seconds he was calm again. They all followed Lila down to the basement they were all confused. Lila rushed to the back of the basement where the rotting cupboard is and moved it to reveal an endless passageway.

"Let's go then." Jason spoke quickly while pushing them in.

The unilluminated length of the tunnel was frightening. It went silent none of them knew what to say and they were all clueless to where they were walking to.

A torch light shone ahead of them Lila stopped this was the first time she had ever panicked because for once she had something to lose. They all slowly turned around to their surprise it was only Noah and Melanie.

"I found this in the bag I was carrying." The young boy whispered.

The walls were covered in old posters and spray paint. They read 'rebellion is the only thing that keeps you alive' another one read 'you can kill a rebel, but you can't kill the rebellion.' This must have been one of the tunnels that the rebels used but they were wrong they could kill the rebellion and they did. There are still a few but everyone is too scared to even dare do anything like that again.

"I know where this is headed." Jordan shouts with joy. "All of the rebellion tunnels finish at the old railway station." At least we know where not headed straight to death Blake thought to himself. After a few hours, they could finally see light at the end of the tunnel Noah got too tired after few hours, so Blake had to carry him. There were a couple of steps leading up to the light. The sun was setting, and it was dark Blake carried Noah to the side of the track and placed him up against the tree.

He looked peaceful, Melanie went over to him and fell asleep next to him.

"We will take it in turns of taking watch" Jason says, he can hardly keep his eyes open whereas I am wide awake.

"I'll take first watch" Lila spoke quietly.

"I'll take second and Jordan will take third" Blake says. They all fall asleep quite quickly it was nice but not exactly peaceful because everyone knows that they might have to wake up in seconds and either run or fight. There was nowhere for them to go to this was their life even if they knew it was ending soon.

Chapter 18

A Form of Trust

Lila woke Blake up because it was his turn to watch but she was unable to get to sleep. The moonlight was the only source of light they had even then it was still hard to see.

"If you could change one thing about this situation, what would you change?" She asks me, to be honest nothing much.

"Depending, if I changed one thing like there was no blue and purple would we all have still met?" Blake questioned.

"Probably not." She whispers. I wouldn't change a thing because I couldn't live a life without these people even Jason and Jordan who have only been here for a day. I think they will stick around though Blake thought thoroughly.

"Then no" She looked surprised to the fact that he wouldn't change a thing.

"I thought you didn't trust any of us." She answers. Blake didn't know who to trust he trusted his family and they turned on him within seconds he always felt like they hadn't ever given a second thought about him.

Eventually Lila fell asleep but Blake still couldn't, so he stayed awake. His whole life had changed, Blake had never been more unsure of his life then this point in time.

The sun rose quite quickly the forest looked as if it was dancing in the wind. Although no matter how beautiful the morning was it couldn't hide all the ugliness in the world.

The others had either went on a walk to try get some more supplies or went back down to the river. Other than Noah he was sat up against a crooked tree. He had always felt out of place even when it was only him and his sister but now, he didn't even feel like he was needed just an extra mouth to feed. Noah knew the others loved him and it wasn't their fault that he was this unhappy. There is only one goal Noah has in life and that is to grow old in a safe place but even the growing old bit seems impossible.

Part Four
The Odds Are Stacked Against Us

Chapter 19

Meanwhile at the guard...All the Odds against Us

A girl with pale white skin with shoulder length black hair sat silently in her prison. For once she was the only one trapped in the hell hole, the rest were dead. She was always left alone the one question that replayed in her mind was 'why am I still alive?'. Most people are only here for a week or two and then they are killed off whereas she has been trapped here for over a year. It's even hard to keep track of time in this place the only source of light in 'The Gaol' is the small lantern that is kept in the middle of 'The Gaol' lucky enough for her she's in the centre. The cobbled walls are as cold as ice. The girl is restricted to only half a slice of bread and one and a half glass of water. Even when 'The Gaol' is empty she cans still here the screams of the dead.

If she wasn't as weak, she would've escaped months ago even if it felt like all the odds were against her, she still would've tried. It's a very old-fashioned place 'The Gaol' most people think that it would be updated with the highest tech, but it is still the hardest thing to escape.

There was always an eerie chill in the air it was as if the world knew the pain surrounding the purples.

There were certain rules in 'The Gaol'. Don't speak unless spoken too and don't look the soldiers in the eye. There's only so much a person can go through before they go insane, but the girl wouldn't class herself as insane more like on the edge.

She used to have a roommate but he abandoned her sometimes she thinks that's why she's still here just in case they come back for her, but she knew long ago that they weren't coming back for her.

She remembers that day as if it were yesterday no matter how much they had argued she would never have left him but that was the difference between them.

Without a warning, the sound of the creaking door echoed throughout 'The Gaol'. It was as if it were instinct the girl stood up abruptly both arms against her side. Unknown of what could happen within the next five minutes. The girl watched silently as another young girl was dragged across the floor her was dragged into the cell next to her the girl's long brown curly hair trailed behind her. The girl was covered in bruises and had a scar across her face, which looked quite new.

The guards attached the new girl's wrist to the ice-cold bar. As soon as the guards left the new girl opened her eyes to reveal soft yellow and brown colour.

"Hello?" The new girl asked in fear. She then said in a hushed tone "I'm Brooklyn." The girl spoke while trying to hide the pain.

The other girl hadn't spoken in months she didn't want to get too attached to Brooklyn, so she kept silent.

"Don't speak then." Brooklyn spoke angrily.

"Isabella. My --- name is ----- Isabella." The girl spoke in a croaky tone.

The guards had no information on Isabella other than her name. Brooklyn couldn't help but think what had happened to Jason and Jordan.

"How long have you been stuck here." Brooklyn spoke quietly. Isabella lost track of time a long time ago, but she knew it was some time over a year.

"About a year and a half." Isabella spoke nervously as she looked down at the floor. Brooklyn was shocked she knew they usually kill them after two weeks or so.

"That long!" Brooklyn exclaimed.

The sound of screams echoed through the cells 'The Gaol' filled with fear. Isabella's facial expression had changed did this mean there finally going to kill me she thought. Brooklyn looked Isabella dead in the eyes Brooklyn watched as Isabella's facial expressions changed Brooklyn then thought this is the end if this had happened two weeks ago, I wouldn't have been bothered but now I'm leaving people behind, I can't do that I need to survive this somehow.

Blood was flowing through the door as if it was the river of death. Suddenly, the electronic locks on the doors and cuffs opened.

They both looked as shocked as each other. The door at the end of 'The Gaol' opened Isabella and Brooklyn instantly moved to the back of the cell to try stay out of sight but they both knew as soon as someone walked through, they would be seen within seconds.

The last gunshot went off and then loud footsteps were walking closer and closer to their cell.

Chapter 20

In a world full of strangers

The footsteps stopped and the cell before. Their hearts both stopped they could see the shadow of the killer.

"ISABELLA!" The killer shouted at them.

Isabella's face went as pale as a ghost the thought of being sick clouded her mind. What do they want with me she thought to herself. Brooklyn felt her eyes getting heavier and heavier she didn't know how long she had till she collapsed. It was as if the room was getting darker by the second Brooklyn thought to herself.

"Brooklyn." Isabella shouted while trying to shake her new friend awake. The killer rushed into the cell. Without thinking the killer ran over to Brooklyn to make sure she was still breathing. Isabella crawled to the other side of the cell.

"Are you okay?" The killer spoke in a calming tone while trying to walk over to Isabella. The girl walked as far away from him as possible, so he turned back around. Silently, Isabella watched as the killer carefully picked Brooklyn up.

"Are you coming or do you want to die here." The killer said harshly. Isabella watched as the man walked out. Then she stood up Isabella didn't want to know what the future held for her, but she knew exactly what would happen if she stayed.

"You came." He spoke in a surprised tone she could tell he was being sarcastic though.

"If you even dare try to kill or hurt us in any way, I will have your head." Isabella threatened the killer.

The killer rolled his eyes he knew there was no way she was being serious he could hardly keep a straight face. They both rushed over to the first gate lucky enough for them it wasn't locked. He must have done this before Isabella thought too herself but how?

Without a warning the sirens started blasting through the speakers and the shutters the killer slowly turned around to face Isabella the look on his face had changed.

Brooklyn was still out cold but the other two just stood there it felt like everything around them was collapsing.

Isabella sprinted to the end of the hall to try open the barricades, but they didn't seem to move at all.

From where Isabella was standing the killer looked like he had all but given up fighting against them. The killer had carefully placed Brooklyn on the floor next to him, but he didn't say a word he just stared at the celling helplessly as if his whole world was crashing down on him which it was.

The killer was speaking under his breath, but Isabella couldn't hear a word he was saying. Isabella couldn't stand still she kept reminding herself that they wouldn't kill her, but she wasn't exactly sure anymore.

"Will you just stay still for more than two seconds?" The killer blurted out angrily.

"No this isn't the end of us. Right?" Isabella spoke quietly as she slowly sat on the ground next to Brooklyn.

The most painful silence surrounded them. The killer had no words to answer the girl's fatal question.

The sirens were still blaring off in a matter of minutes the cells would be filled with hundreds off guards and all their chances of escaping would vanish.

"What's your favourite colour? Mines mint green." Isabella spoke softly while trying to hide the tears in her eyes. Isabella still wasn't used to speaking to people, but she refuses to die without having a real conversation with someone.

"When we get out of here, I will tell you along with my name but until then we're strangers." The killer spoke with a hint of hope in his voice.

The sirens stopped and the whole room fell silent, only for a matter of moments the whole room felt empty. The moment was gone within seconds, but it felt like a lifetime.

"We're waiting for death." Isabella spoke impatiently.

"Yeah." The killer answered quickly.

The sound of running guards echoed throughout 'The Gaol'

Brooklyn's eyes flickered open.

"Where am I?" Brooklyn asked in a croaky voice. But deep-down Brooklyn knew exactly where she was, but she didn't want to admit it.

"Take a guess." The killer said bluntly.

"Wait do you hear that." Isabella interrupted them.

All three of them jumped up and ran over to window that had iron metal bars on the outside. Neither of them could believe what they were seeing, the royal flags which could only mean one thing the king was here to view an execution.

"He is not going to be happy. I killed about fifty of his guards." The killer spoke while nervously laughing.

Isabella had never seen the king not exactly anyway she had heard that he had visited a few times and he had walked past her once, but she averted her eyes to floor. His nickname is the King of death, and it is said that the souls that he has tortured follow in his path.

All three of them knew that this was the end none of them were exactly sure how this would go down, but they knew by this time tomorrow they would all surely be dead.

The three could hear the king's deadly voice through the floor they all heard the gunshots. It was within a second, they heard the bodies hit the ice-cold floor.

"I want whoever did this now." The king demanded.

Without a warning, Brooklyn grabbed Isabella and the killer's arms. The killer tried to talk but Brooklyn stopped him, "Look." Brooklyn whispered while pointing to the carriage.

"And?" The killer spoke in an annoyed tone.

"If you get me to there, I can get us out of 'The Gaol'.

Isabella crawled to the doorway none of the guards would have expected us to have stayed in the cells it's a perfect plan Isabella thought to herself.

"Come on then." Isabella mumbled.

The king's deadly voice echoed throughout 'The Gaol' but he wasn't alone. He was accompanied by his eldest daughter who was next in line for the crown. But everyone knew that she would never be queen the king is never going to allow for his crown to be passed to her, so he makes it look as if she doesn't want the crown, instead of admitting what his true beliefs are.

"What are you three doing here?" A voice spoke in a loud tone.

The killer and Brooklyn spun around to see who the voice had come from, but Isabella didn't need to turn around she knew exactly who it was.

Alexandra Rose as in the king's daughter.

"Isabella, we meet again." Alexandra spoke in a posh tone.

The killer glared at Isabella as if it to say what the hell have you done and why is it going to get me killed.

"Alex." Isabella said while turning around. "Miss me." Isabella said while leaning into hug her.

"Of course." Alexandra spoke quickly.

The killer couldn't get over how bizarre this all was his mind kept going back to the same subjects why hadn't she killed us yet or why hasn't she sent someone to kill us.

"Why are you here?" Isabella whispered.

The princess' face had changed to a totally different emotion it looked more like fear from where Brooklyn was standing. The killer didn't want to turn he could sense someone was behind him. Out of the three of them the killer was the only one who felt sick over the fact that he was going to die here. The others had gotten used to the fact that this very well may be the place they take their last breath.

"Your highness---." The guard didn't even get to finish his sentence before Alexandra killed him.

"Come on then we don't have all day." The princess said within a second.

Alexandra passed a gun to the killer before they headed for the backdoor. Getting out of the world's longest maze would be easier than getting out of The Gaol'.

There was an armed guard at every corner even more now since the killer had shot about fifty of them.

Alexandra leaded them towards a basement.

"What's your name?" Alexandra mumbled while pointing at the killer.

"Greyson." He said softly.

"Here's the plan Greyson is going to go and distract the guards and by distract, I mean kill." Alexandra spoke in a deadly tone.

"I like you already." Greyson laughed.

Isabella couldn't help but think this was a bad idea and how bad it was going to be when they get caught.

"Will you be quiet Isabella?" Greyson demanded.

"I didn't say anything." Isabella complained.

"Well, stop thinking so loudly then." Greyson whispered angrily.

Alexandra looked at Isabella is if to say it will be fine, we will all get out of this alive, but it didn't reassure her at all in fact it made her worry more.

Brooklyn was awfully silent given the fact that they are destined to die at any moment.

Without a second to lose Greyson barged into the basement and shot all five of the armed guards dead.

"Come on then." The killer spoke in a rushed tone.

The three rushed down the stairs and into the basement the three of them looked at Alexander eager for her to tell them how they are going to get out of there.

"Follow me." Alexandra whispered.

Isabella couldn't help but glance back at the stairs it was as if she could feel the guards getting closer it wasn't until Greyson tugged on her arm till, she stopped watching the stairs.

"We don't have all day." The killer spoke in a rushed tone.

None of them knew where Alexandra was leading them to.

The gun shots still echoed throughout The Guard they all knew there was no turning back now.

It was as if their lives were balancing on a strand of string if they make one wrong move there all dead.

Chapter 21

The Other Side

Alexandra's mind was racing she couldn't help but think if she had made the wrong decision, but she sharply snapped out of it. She knew her doubting herself would only slow them down what didn't help was they all depended on her for their survival.

"Alexandra, do you have any clue to where we are going?" Brooklyn asked in a worried tone.

But she didn't answer it was as if she wasn't even in the same room as them, but she knew exactly where they were going.

The basement stretched out the full length and width of The Guard.

Greyson's head wasn't in the right place either but then again none of them were.

"Quickly, grab the candle stick that's attach to the wall. I will meet you on the other side." Alexandra spoke in a hurried tone.

"You're leaving us." Greyson spoke bluntly. "How do we know this isn't a trap?"

Alexandra stopped walking and turned around. Isabella had already pulled the candle stick which revealed a tunnel. It looks as if it could be a murder passage Isabella thought.

"She trusts me, whether you do or not I don't care I'm doing this for her. So, stay or go see if I care." Alexandra angrily whispered while pointing at Isabella.

Tears were forming in Isabella's eyes, but she wasn't going to let the rest of them realise but she wasn't sure whether to trust Alexandra or not she is the king's daughter.

"Fine." Greyson spoke in a hurt tone.

Just like that Alexandra vanished shocking both Greyson and Brooklyn but not Isabella she knew Alexandra would come back.

The tunnel was covered in mud.

"I guess this is a bad time to mention I'm claustrophobic." Brooklyn's voice echoed through.

"You'll be fine." Greyson said while crawling through the tunnel.

You'll be fine you'll be fine Brooklyn repeated in her head as she got onto her knees, she quickly changed her mind and jumped up.

"Brooklyn, close your eyes and follow my voice." Greyson whispered.

Brooklyn followed his voice and kept her eyes shut tight.

"You're on a beach drinking a margarita." Greyson spoke in a soothing tone.

"I've never had a margarita." Isabella added.

Greyson grabbed a hold of Brooklyn's hand he could tell this was her worst fear, but he kept reassuring her that they would make it out alive.

"Open your eyes." He spoke softly to Brooklyn.

She opened them streaks of light were peering into the tunnel.

"Quickly." Alexandra spoke in a rushed tone while helping them out of the tunnel.

"You can ride horses right." Alexandra inquired.

"Sort off." Greyson answered.

Alexandra sprinted back to where she had come from. Brooklyn could still hear the marching in the background that had echoed the halls of the guard.

Isabella looked around the corner which revealed one of the training centres. Boys and girls not older than 12 were learning to fight just the thought of the blues children, being turned into killing machines saddened them all.

"Better too not think about." Greyson whispered.

Isabella turned back around to her surprise Alexandra had come back with two horses.

One of the horses was grey with white speckled dots. The other one was a caramel colour with a white nose.

"The grey horse is called Izzy and the other one is called Holly." Alexandra spoke while turning around to face them.

Brooklyn looked back at Isabella and the girl could tell that Isabella was uncomfortable, but Brooklyn had too much to worry about.

The alarms had stopped.

Chapter 22

Runaway

"Quickly, Isabella you're with me. Greyson you're with Brooklyn. If we lose each other keep heading north."

None of them had time to agree or disagree the alarms had stopped which could only mean one thing they knew where they were.

Holly was the fastest by a mile off it was Izzy that was struggling to catch up.

Greyson and Brooklyn looked lie small figures in the distance none of them planned on looking back not until they were at least seventy miles away from The Gaol'.

"Seriously, Izzy." Isabella spoke in angry tone.

Alexandra kept her eyes straight at the road she was going to do everything in her power to avoid this conversation.

"So, you're ignoring me now, classic." Isabella spoke in a sarcastic tone.

"Classic how is that classic." Alexandra screamed.

Isabella jumped off the horse and started running.

"Now this is classic. Her running away from her problems." Alexandra mumbled under her breath.

Alexandra stayed far behind Isabella.

Greyson and Brooklyn were still miles ahead of Alexandra and Isabella.

"What do you think happened between them?" Greyson questioned.

"Honestly, relationship issues." Brooklyn spoke without even thinking too deeply about it.

"I guess it makes sense." Greyson said.

"Isabella get back on the horse!" Alexandra demanded impatiently.

Isabella didn't even look back at her she couldn't go back through the pain of loving her.

Isabella stood still looking through the overgrown field. The ancient black dress had stayed with her the full way through her time in The Gaol'. It was hardly a dress now it was covered in holes and the skirt had a slit going through it.

Alexandra had jumped off the horse and stood behind Isabella.

"I'm sorry." Alexandra spoke quietly.

Isabella kept looking forward at the sunset the sky was a reddish pink colour the sky did not mirror their situation at all.

"Just get back on the horse I promise I won't say anything." Alexandra spoke in a promising tone.

Eventually, they both got back on the horse.

The princess kept her promise and didn't say a word no matter how much she longed to speak to Isabella. Alexandra had promised herself she wouldn't hurt her ever again.

The sky had already turned to night. But this night was no different to any other night it was freezing and too dark to see anything more than two feet in front of them.

"What's that?" Isabella spoke in a worried tone while pointing into the distance.

In the distance there was a small flame which lit up the near surroundings it was quite near the old train station.

"I don't know. It could either be another runaway group or it could be a trap. Should we take the chance?" Alexandra asked Isabella.

"We should check it out just in case. Plus, what if Greyson and Brooklyn took that path and it is a trap." Isabella whispered.

After thinking deeply about all the cons and pros of taking the path or leaving the others behind.

"Fine." Alexandra spoke quickly.

Chapter 23

In the Shadows

Everyone else was asleep other than Lila it was her turn to keep a look out for any chance of danger. But she didn't plan on sleeping anyway her mind was all over the place she couldn't help but think of all the bad things that were going to happen.

Blake's snoring echoed throughout the camp.

"Brooklyn, we don't even know where we're going the light could just be a trap you don't know the lengths they will go to." Greyson spoke in a faint tone.

"Blake! Blake! wake up." Lila spoke in a worried tone while shaking him to try wake him up.

Blake's eyes shot open he could tell by Lila's facial expressions that something terrible had happened or was about to happen that he wasn't sure about.

"What's going on?" Blake spoke in a rushed tone while trying to sit up.

"There's someone over there." She whispered while pointing at the shadows.

"Wake up the others." Blake spoke quietly while reaching for his gun.

Lila had woken everyone else up the shadows were still talking but not loud enough for them to hear what they were talking about.

Melanie tried to walk closer to Blake but Jason pulled her back behind him if anyone was going to make it out of this it would be Noah and Melanie, he thought to himself while pulling his gun out.

Another horse sprinted towards the shadows. The voices had gotten louder but they could still only the odd word.

"Quickly, get behind the bushes." Blake rushed through his words like there was no tomorrow which is how it felt for every single one of them.

None of them were thinking they would make another day. At least I'm not dying alone Jordan thought to herself.

Reluctantly they all listened to Blake and had concealed themselves behind the bushes.

"What if we don't make it?" Noah spoke in a scared tone.

Jordan leaned into hug the young boy she had no idea what to tell him even she didn't think they would survive the night.

"Then we get to go to a better place far away from all of this mess.." She whispered to try and calm the child down.

A shadowed figure walked along side to horses and tied them to the tree.

The figure hand motioned the other three shadows to join them.

Without a warning Blake abruptly stood up and pointed his gun at them which caused Jason and Jordan to do the same.

"Who are you?" Blake roared.

The three figures turned around to their surprise it was not a trap.

"Mate chill you nearly give me a heart attack." Greyson said calmly.

It couldn't be Melanie thought to herself.

"Greyson?" Blake hesitated.

"The one and only." Greyson confirmed.

Without hesitating Blake sprinted over and hugged his best friend.

"You'll never guess who I found." Greyson informed Blake.

Who could he have that I know Blake thought to himself?

Isabella stepped out of the shadows Blake's facial expression had changed.

"Isabella I'm sorry." But she cut him off but instead of yelling at him she hugged him.

They didn't get along not at all when they were locked up together. They drove each other insane and they will end up hating each other, but in this moment, they were just glad both were safe at least for now.

"I still hate you by the way." She spoke while breaking up the hug. She then said "I need the rest of you not to panic I promise you aren't in any danger."

The rest of the group stood up quickly and moved over to Blake.

"What do you mean don't panic why would we panic." Melanie spoke in a concerned tone.

"This is Brooklyn and Alexandra."

Jason and Jordan ran over to Brooklyn and hugged her they were so relieved that she was alright now.

"Wait Alexandra as in the Princess Alexandra." Lila shouted.

Their facial expressions changed from relieved to pure horror. Melanie grabbed a hold of her brother and stepped in front of him she was planning on protecting him till the day she dies.

"I swear on my life. I am not here to hurt you. I'm like you." Alexandra spoke while lifting her sleeve.

Jason's jaw dropped he

"Alexandra you're still alive." Blake spoke in a fake disappointing voice.

"Blake I'm sorry but I can't change what I did." Alexandra cried.

There were tears in her eyes but Blake didn't change.

"Blake, I don't know what she did but can it wait my head is slowly killing me." Greyson exaggerated.

"Fine but tomorrow we talk about it." Blake hissed.

Blake tried to stay up but Jordan insisted that he got some rest she knew tomorrow was going to be a terrible and long day but she couldn't sleep. So, she decided to take Blake's place and stay up for look out.

Jordan had always imagined that the stars that lit up the sky were the purples that had been murdered.

It was as if there dead souls lit up the night sky.

Chapter 24
Wating for death

The sun rose quite quickly but the air was still cold. The trees were blocking out the sun creating massive shadows.

"Jordan." Noah said.

Everyone else was still fast asleep. But they're going to have to wake up soon Jordan thought to herself.

"Are you feeling better today?" Jordan asked him.

"I don't know I still have the feeling something terrible is about to happen." Noah blurted out.

Jordan felt guilty over the fact that she couldn't control what was happening around her or guarantee any of them even having a future.

"Go and wake up the others." Jordan spoke while walking back over to the horse.

Without thinking Noah ran over to Brooklyn and started to wake her up.

Jordan stood staring at the ground with tears flowing down her face.

"You okay." Blake spoke softly.

"Yes, I'm fine." She spoke while quickly trying to wipe her tears while trying to not bring to much attention to herself.

"No, you're not." He whispered.

Slowly she turned around to face him but to her surprise he hugged her. It was as if she collapsed in his arms, he couldn't help but breakdown as well. Their full lives were on the line every waking moment and they had no energy left to fight them. But they weren't going to stop fighting not until their very last breath.

After about five minutes everyone else was already awake but they were nowhere near ready especially not for the fight ahead.

"Ready." Blake asked while pulling away from the hug.

"As ready as I'll ever be." Jordan answered with a quick smile.

Jason and Greyson had gone off hunting to see if they could catch anything. Noah was climbing the trees with Jordan; they had decided to keep him a child for as long as possible even though he was already aware of most of the treacherous things that were happening around him.

Lila was sitting next to the fire she was the only one who was a good cook out of the eleven of them.

"Do you think he will be mad at me forever?" Alexandra spoke while sitting next to Lila.

She looked up at her Lila knew she would never fully trust Alexandra even if she was a purple.

"Depends on what you did. But given his reaction I would say yes he will be angry at you forever." Lila spoke while staring at the ground.

"This is the last night we're staying here just in case you didn't know. I would highly recommend staying awake because I don't think they will wake you up to come with us." Lila warned Alexandra.

Lila ran over to Melanie smiling.

Alexandra knew they were always going to leave her out but she was nowhere near expecting Blake to be here. She broke his and Isabella's trust, she had vowed to keep them safe even if they wish her dead up until the day she dies.

"You wouldn't mind." Melanie spoke while handing Lila a bobble.

"Sure." Lila spoke with a smile on her face.

Melanie had the longest and messiest brown curly hair. Lila tried her best to plait it but it was still very untidy but that was the last thing on anyone's mind.

Blake stayed a far distance from Alexandra he couldn't shake the feeling that something was about to happen but he couldn't quite grasp it.

Greyson and Jason came back not long after four o clock. They had only caught three pheasants which was not even enough food for four of them.

"Isabella, can you do me a quick favour and go fill up theses buckets of water." Greyson asked her.

She nodded it didn't take her too long to collect the water. Lila and Jordan had already started cooking the food. Everyone felt exhausted by the time the food was cooked.

Isabella was given the most since she had been half starved for the past few years.

It was Greyson's turn to keep watch out tonight even though he was shattered he did his best to keep his eyes wide open.

Chapter 25

Time doesn't fly by

As soon as morning hit, they were all up. There was no chance of them surviving here.

Noah and Greyson were on one horse and Melanie and Alexandra were on the other.

"Where are we headed?" Greyson shouted back at Blake.

"Just keep heading south." Blake yelled while passing him one of the compasses.

Blake kept his eyes on Melanie the whole time he didn't trust Alexandra one bit.

"Do any of you have even the slightest idea to where we are going to go?" Lila asked them.

"We could go to the south harbour and steal a boat. I know this one place where we would be safe for a bit. But it is a few days travel and that's on a horse so it might take weeks." Alexandra advised.

"We surviving more than two days will shock me." Blake announced.

Only Greyson was shocked to Blake's comment.

"We survived months on the road when we were searching for Melanie and Noah so yes, we will make it." Greyson pointed out.

Blake went silent quickly he wasn't going to argue with Greyson.

A few weeks on the road might be the thing that kills me Isabella thought to herself.

The silence was starting to make them all paranoid Greyson was checking behind him less than every two seconds. Whereas Lila couldn't help but feel like guards were going to charge at them at every moment.

Noah was the only one who could rest he didn't worry as much as the others but that was only because of his age. He would soon realise that his life isn't as fun and joyful as it's led out to be.

Melanie was the opposite she knew all the ins and outs of the world's darkest shames. She had never been hidden from the world, but she would spend the rest of her life hiding it from him.

"How long till we stop." Jason complained.

"Stop complaining we will stop in a few hours." Greyson spoke annoyed.

Should I be helping them they could be leading me to my downfall this could be the end of me, if my farther finds out I have disobeyed him he will throw me to the wolves for my head Alexandra thought deeply.

"I'm sorry but I can't do this helping you could lead me to my own death." Alexandra announced.

"Don't you dare?" Isabella yelled.

But it was too late she had already dashed into the woods it looked as if she had vanished, she had gone that fast.

"Melanie." Noah screamed.

"Run after them then." Blake shouted at them all.

Blake refused to let her ruin one more thing in his life.

By the time they had started running after them Alexandra and Noah were already deep into the woods.

"Take me back." Melanie cried.

Alexandra had totally forgotten that she had Noah with her but there was no chance in hell she was going to take him back.

"I'm sorry child but you're going to have to stay here." Alexandra spoke in a threatening tone while dragging Melanie off the horse.

Alexandra looked into Melanie's desperate eyes but something kept her in place. She wasn't heartless but she didn't want to die.

Death can bring out the worst in some people but it can also bring out the best in others.

Suddenly the sound of marching echoed throughout the forest. There was nowhere to go. Melanie tried to run but the grip of Alexandra's hand on the back of her neck had tightened.

Within seconds they were surrounded, Melanie couldn't tell if Alexandra was protecting her or trying to get her killed. But it wasn't long till she knew that Alexandra wanted her dead.

The Guards had tied them both to the stump of the trees. Tears were falling quickly down Melanie's face she wasn't ready to die but what hurt her even more was the fact that she was going to die alone.

Their black suits made them look like they were being controlled Melanie always found it easier to imagine that they weren't people underneath their mask more like mind-controlled robots.

"I beg of you. Please don't kill me." Alexandra begged

"Please help me." One of the guards mocked her.

She looked up at them with tears in her eyes. One of the guards turned back to Melanie and kicked her in the stomach.

She bowed her head to hide the tears that threatened to overflow "Has the king said anything?"

"No." The guard towering over her said.

The guard turned back to Melanie with a horrifying smirk painted across his face.

"Any last words." The guard threatened.

"God praise the revolution." Melanie shouted.

One of the guards placed the cold metal gun against the Melanie's head but they didn't look back at her it was as if they had a slight feeling of remorse.

The first time I've ever saw a guard showing human emotions and I'm going to die Melanie thought rapidly.

Pow!

The gun shot went off, but Melanie still felt alive she wasn't quite sure whether she was dead or alive.

"Melanie." Noah screamed again.

Melanie opened her eyes to reveal her petrified brother without even giving her a minute to open her eyes fully, he had already pulled her into a hug.

Blake's face had turned red, bright red. It was as if his anger was taking over him, he didn't know how long he would be able to control it. Then, he lost it. He lunged towards her. He dragged her towards the tree.

Alexandra's face was turning pale. Her breathing was increasing and she could begin to hear her heart beating.

"Plea- Plea- Pleas-Please." Alexandra stuttered.

"What? Don't kill you." Blake laughed.

Jason ran over to Melanie trying to get her to sit up. Isabella didn't know where to place herself, she watched as Blake towered over Alexandra. Isabella knew he wouldn't control his anger for much longer.

His mind was in a battle. He wasn't sure whether to kill her or leave her. No matter what choice he chose he knew he would regret it later.

"Blake don't." Isabella pleaded.

Blake couldn't help but fill up with rage it was as if the whole world weren't seeing what was straight in front of them. But his mind was so indecisive he didn't want to make a wrong move. It was as if he were playing a game of chess either decision can affect the entire game. Will he win or will he loose?

"She tried to kill Melanie." Blake screamed while stepping over one of the guard's lifeless bodies. "She could've gotten us all killed."

Isabella had no words she wanted to say Alexandra didn't deserve it but that wasn't exactly true.

"Can I at least punch her in the face?" Blake asked her.

"No." Isabella rolled her eyes.

"What if I just break her nose a little bit?" Blake threatened while towering over Alexandra.

Isabella just turned around and walked back to the road she could feel the tears rushing down her face. Even though she didn't trust Alexandra she could never in her wildest dreams imagined she would've done this.

"Did you kill her?" Isabella whispered while wiping her tears away.

Greyson carried Melanie back onto the horse. They were all exhausted and clueless of what was going to happen next.

"No, I didn't but she will die there." Blake said.

That was it there were no conversations none of them had anything to say to one another. A few of them already had expected something like this to happen but none of them really thought much about what would happen.

The guilt was slowly eating away at Brooklyn even though she didn't really speak to Alexandra, but she knew if she brought up any conversation on the situation, they would all turn on her in a matter of minutes.

Greyson didn't want to leave Alexandra either, but he knew what Blake and Isabella would've said if he had even thought about it, so he tried his best to keep Alexandra out of his mind.

Eventually they stopped walking. They set up camp not too far away from the road but far enough for nobody to see them.

Star struck; Lila stopped to watch the stunning colours painted across the sky slowly disappearing into nothing.

Jason was the only one who wasn't bothered about tomorrow he had always been taught to live in the present and that is what he was doing. Even if the moment was so dull that he would much rather pass out he would stay and see it through.

"We should talk." Jordan said while trying to break the uncomfortable silence.

"Where are we headed?" Lila questioned.

They all looked at Blake as if he were the key to all their answers.

"Where not headed anywhere." Blake stated.

"What was the point in running if none of you have a plan? We're dancing with death. One minute we're praying that we're not going to die and the next minute when you're safe you don't seem to care." Greyson blurted out.

Melanie kept staring at the ground trying to avoid any of the awkward conversations. Deep down though she knew he was right she knew one day she would be killed but would that day be soon that was what she wondered.

"Your right." Jason spoke. "But what is the point in living for tomorrow if you live for today nobody will care what happens tomorrow or the day after that."

"So, what's the plan Blake?" Lila asked him.

All eyes were on him even though he didn't want it truth is he had no plan, but he wasn't going to admit that they all needed him for a chance at survival.

Chapter 26

Heading South

"We keep heading south it's our only chance." Blake told them.

A chance at survival was all they had asked for. Blake had never understood the word hope not until this day anyway he always thought it was a religious word that only meant something to the blues. Although now hope felt like his safe place but not only his safe place but everyone who was around him.

The second Alexandra had run off with Melanie, Blake felt like his whole world had shattered into a million pieces. Even though he would have much preferred to have seen Alexandra suffer. He couldn't have put Isabella through any more pain no matter how much he despised her.

Isabella on the other hand didn't hate him even though she longed to. It was as if even before she realised the bond they all shared deep down she knew they would eventually be like family.

They all were part of it even if they weren't sure of what it meant but they would soon find out.

"Do you think any of us will truly find peace?" Greyson questioned hopefully.

"It may not seem like it, but most would say this is quite peaceful."

They all nodded in agreement.

"For once no one's trying to kill us." Jason gasped dramatically. He then said, "At least not this minute."

"How long do you think it will be till they catch up with us?" Melanie whispered.

"Longer than we think." Jordan whispered.

Eventually most of them drifted off to sleep except Isabella she had to keep watch. Blake had already addressed to Noah's injuries they weren't too bad, but they could all tell the boy was in pain.

"Why did you keep that?" Blake said while pointing at the leather necklace.

Isabella glanced down at the necklace she remembered that day as if it were yesterday. One of the guards had handed it to her the day Blake had disappeared.

"It reminded me of you."

They both knew in a matter of minutes everyone would be awake and ready to set off.

"But you left me and I don't think I will ever be able to forgive you." Isabella spoke in a hurt tone.

Blake rolled his eyes she knew he had no choice but he couldn't care less what she thought about him.

They had to leave no matter how safe they felt it would only be a matter of hours till they were discovered.

To stay undiscovered that was the plan no matter who twisted it or what happened that was the plan.

Their minds were all preoccupied on surviving nothing less and nothing more.

The sky's most enchanting colours painted the sky that night scarlet red and a pale pink collided in the sky. The clouds were perfectly in line with the sky. It was what Jordan had imagined heaven to be like she wasn't one to believe in religion but she believed that there is a heaven and a hell.

"It's beautiful isn't it?" Jordan said.

Greyson looked up but for only a moment he wanted to keep his focus on surviving the day.

"If only we had to time to enjoy the wonders the world has to offer." Jason spoke softly.

It was as if the scarlet red in the clouds represent the losses that the world suffers through each day.

Chapter 27
A feeling of death

Lila's leg had totally given up she shouldn't have kept walking on it but she had no choice, she just had to battle through the pain. Most of them had been seriously injured over the past month but the one person they were all worried about was Melanie none of them knew how badly she had taken the hit to the stomach not yet anyways. The south harbour was a far journey but not even one of them complained.

My legs are killing me but if I bring it up Blake will never let me hear the end of it Lila thought.

Like a bud opening in the spring happiness blossomed inside Noah, he knew there was a lot to be depressed about but they were all together and in them few moments he was the happiest he had ever been. On the other hand, Blake wasn't happy he was anything but, he knew this moment was going to end in a few minutes but he didn't know how.

"I can't wait to get on a boat and leave this place." Noah exclaimed.

Blake pulled a quick smile on his face but anyone who looked for longer than a minute could tell that it was fake. Isabella noticed but she wasn't going to mention it being stuck in a cell with him for more than two years she learned that he was not one to talk about feelings.

They hadn't even reached the harbour yet but the panic had already set in, it was as if he knew they should avoid the harbour at all costs but deep down he knew it was there only chance. Despite, Blake feeling like he is being lured to his death he noticed that he wasn't the only one battling with their emotions.

Isabella also had a terrible feeling in fact it wasn't a feeling more of a terrifying thought. She couldn't help but imagine the worst she zoned out into her own imagination, but it wasn't exactly clear what she was viewing.

Like a bird she floated above the harbour she saw that the guards were surrounding it. At that moment she knew where they were headed was going to be a blood bath.

"Are you sure heading this way is a good idea." Isabella muttered to Blake

Deep down he wanted to say you have that feeling to but he knew it would only rise panic between them and he was panicking enough for the full group, more panic would just create a chaotic mess.

"It's our best shot." Blake forced a smile.

Isabella was torn between two worlds reality and the reality she feared the most. It was these moments where she missed the guard but when she thinks it, she knows the rest of the group would think she had lost the plot. It was as if the Guard give her some sort of fake safety and she knew that she knew it was a fake safety but it was better than no safety. Instead of asking Greyson did he feel the same way about The Gaol' she kept her mouth shut. She didn't want to bring up anymore awkward conversations.

For Isabella and Blake, it felt like it took minutes to get there whereas for Jordan and Brooklyn it felt like it had taken years to get there.

The sea wind was wild it was as if it were hitting them in the face Greyson took it as a sign that they should leave but he didn't want to give anyone doubtful thoughts.

Surprisingly, Isabella's imagination was right guards were at every corner and they were only hidden by a prickly bush.

CHAPTER 28

Two Gun Shots

The docks were heavily guarded there must have been at least ten times more guards here then at the market.

They were all dressed in a navy blue which could only mean one thing they were there on official business from the king.

"Blake you may be smart but how the fuck do you think we are just going to sneak past about a thousand guards and steal boat. Which I think is carrying hundreds of weapons especially made for the king." Brooklyn blurted out.

Blake's eyes glared back at her.

"Have you got any good ideas? No didn't think so." Blake hissed.

The whole group fell silent. Jordan was too busy imagining how in the world they were going to get past a single guard never mind stealing one of the most guarded ships.

"All we have to do is wait till it gets dark then there will be definitely less guards." Melanie spoke while staring at her chipped finger nails.

A smile formed on Isabella's face but it wasn't because of what Melanie had said it was due to her caring more about what her finger nails looked like then her life-threatening situation.

"Okay let's go with that." Jason announced.

Gradually the rain was getting heavier and heavier drowning out all the sounds. The gunshots were getting quieter by the second. Even the useless shouts from them were getting fainter. The rain fell from the dark blue sky it looked as if the sky was having its own mental break down but it didn't seem to bother anyone. They were all practically lying down none of them could risk being seen.

The hours of silence took hours but the hell-vans eventually did arrive. For once they weren't capturing innocent people, they were just being used to transport deadly killers.

"Okay, let's go now." Blake rushed.

The docks were still ridiculously guarded but they wouldn't have had another chance. They were already dangerously low on weapons but they still had a fighting chance.

Without a second to lose them slowly made their way closer to the docks. The water was a murky dark blue with a mix of light green. The rain was causing the water level to rise slightly.

The piercing sound of troops marching into battle is what their lethal stomps sounded like. It was as if they had known all along where they were headed but that couldn't have been possible Blake thought breathlessly.

"No- they don't know where here right." Isabella panicked.

Jason nervously laughed trying to ignore the fact that their life is always close to death. It was as if their life was criss-crossing with death at every moment.

Blake's soaking wet hair was covering his eyes but he didn't even have a single moment to care about anything over than their survival.

"Our odds are next to nothing but we must try. If there is even a single chance that at least some of us make it out of here I know it will be the highlight of my life, knowing that the rest of you are safe." Greyson declared.

The marching was getting closer but it still felt like a lifetime away.

"If we go down then we go down together." Lila chanted.

They weren't wrong within seconds fists were flying guns were blaring off. Blood covered the pavement. The guards set off smoke bombs which covered the entire place with thick bright white smoke.

Lila looked badly beaten it was as if her entire life had appeared before her. The Guard placed her against the soaking ground. It was as if her breathing had stopped, she wasn't going to beg for her life but that doesn't mean she didn't want to live it. Blood was flowing from her nose she heard the echoing sirens that flowed from one ear to the other.

"Melanie." Noah screamed.

Jason had already forced Melanie onto the boat he would have gotten Noah as well but the smoke was too heavy for him to see him.

The wind created the rain into bullets piercing their skin at every waking moment.

Gradually, Jordan picked her brick like feet of the ground and ran for her life. Even though she had spent her full life running she had never known what it was like to run when death was inevitably going to happen.

Greyson carried Lila onto the boat. Seconds felt like minutes it was as if everything was in slow motion nothing felt right for any of them. Without thinking Blake sprinted towards the boat while shooting back at two of the guards. There was one guard she was wearing a bullet proof navy uniform that had four white stripes on her left arm. Blake had always found it difficult to believe that there were ever actual people underneath their merciless uniforms. But he didn't stop shooting it was as if something had taken over him. When he was younger, he could never have imagined killing anyone even the ones that were supposed to kill him. Growing up he despised his family for being hostile murders but if he had ever mentioned it, he would have had a bullet put straight through his head.

"Where's Noah? Where's Isabella?" Melanie screamed.

Blake aggressively turned around his eyes searched but the smoke was too heavy bullets were still firing but at that moment he prayed for both. Even Isabella a girl he longed to hate.

He wanted her safe even if it meant she mentally tortured him for the rest of his life.

"Noah." Isabella screamed but not loud enough for anyone to hear.

Her heart was pounding. Her eyes were closing. The room was slowly getting darker.

But no, she wasn't dying. At least not here. Not today she repeated to herself. Gradually she picked herself off the floor first she was going to get Noah and then she was going to leave this part of the country.

Slowly the smoke started to clear a bit but nowhere near enough to see properly.

"Turn around." A deep voice commanded.

Isabella did as he said but she could feel the colour drain from her face as she looked forward. Noah's face was as white as snow and tears were falling quickly down his face.

"It's going to be okay I promise Noah." Isabella said hopelessly.

Within seconds two-gun shots echoed throughout the docks.

Chapter 29

Stay with me... Stay with me

Don't close your eyes stay with me

"No, no, no stay with me stay with me." Isabella screamed.

Without even losing a moment she ran over to Noah as if it was the last thing, she would ever do. It was as if she caught him at the perfect moment, she felt a moment of relief when she heard him breathe even if he was only gasping for breath.

"Where are you?" Blake yelled.

"Were here, were here." Isabella repeated.

Luckily, he heard her but she would never forget the look on his face. But he didn't wait a second, he carefully took Noah from her protecting arms and carried him to safety.

In the next two minutes the people on the boat's lives would change more than any of them could have imagined especially Melanie's.

Isabella couldn't help but believe she could've stopped this if only she had gotten there a moment sooner, he might've had a better chance.

"What- happened." Melanie stuttered.

Blake sat him up against one of the sides of the boat.

"I CAN GET US OUT OF HERE IN ABOUT TWO MINUTES." Greyson shouted.

Noah was bleeding heavily while Blake was trying to staunch the blood but Noah was concerned more about the fact that Melanie is sobbing and panicking.

The boat has already started moving and the uncontrollable winds weren't helping any of them.

"Blake just stop." Noah stated.

His skin was as white as paper and purple circles surrounded his eyes. Noah's lips were chipped and they were the same colour as the circles around his eyes.

"No, you're not dying." Melanie cried while rushing over to him.

Blood was slowly trickling out of the left corner of his small mouth.

"You're only nine you're supposed to have an amazing future." Melanie whispered.

Her heart was slowly breaking. Jordan kneeled beside her and placed her hand on Melanies shoulder. They all either kneeled or sat next to Noah all except Greyson who was steering the ship north. Greyson kept looking back at the deck to see tears and hearts breaking. This is what they do this is what they do to us. The anger in him was building up quickly he felt his hand grip onto the steering wheel as if it were the only thing that was keeping him from breaking the ground beneath him.

"Go." Jason whispered to Greyson.

Helplessly, Jason steered the boat north awaiting the news he feared the most. Although, him and Noah were close he knew he was needed to get them out of there, and the others needed to say goodbye.

"Hey, kid." Greyson whispered while placing a hand on Noah's head.

Tears were falling from Noah's eyes. Greyson was trying to bite back the tears he didn't want the child's last moments to be of him crying.

"I don't want to die please help me." Noah sobbed.

The rain had stopped which made the sky fill with thousands of stars which made the world look peaceful even if that was a lie and the world was the exact opposite.

"Hey buddy look up at the sky and forget everything else that's all you need to focus on." Blake spoke in a comforting tone.

Noah tried to forget but he couldn't but he made it look like he did for Melanie's sake. But he never let go of her hand.

"You stay awake do you hear me?! Don't you dare close your eyes? Please! Come on!" Melanie shook his lifeless body but he didn't move.

She held his body until it went cold but even then, she wouldn't let anyone touch him not even Blake.

They stayed with her a few minutes but they could tell she needed time and space. They could give her space but they didn't know how much time they could give her.

"Blake." Isabella hissed.

Blake followed her to the captain's cabin. The rest of them were stood in a circle half sobbing. Lila had a new scar going across her eye one of the guards had cut her face in the fight.

"What?!" He shouted impatiently.

They all turned around to face him all of them new it except him that he was the leader of them. He made every final decision whether he was aware of it or not. None of them were sure to what they wanted from him but they trusted him.

"What's your plan?" Brooklyn hurried while trying to break the silence.

"My plan. Are you serious I have no idea Noah's dead everything is falling on me well guess what I have no idea for all I know one of you have a key to our survival?" Blake blurted out.

"We could float him into the water with a few flowers surrounding him." Jason sobbed.

"He's not dead stop planning his funeral. This is a dream not a single bit of this is real. I hit my head I don't know but I do know this isn't real." Melanie cried while entering the cabin. They all looked towards her their hearts breaking as she spoke none of them had any words that would help console her.

Blake kneeled next to her with tears overflowing in his eyes he didn't know how to put it but he knew she needed to hear him say the words.

"Noah's dead." He cried.

As soon as Blake had whispered those words, she ran out of the room but Blake slowly followed her. He didn't want her to feel forced into telling him how she felt but he also didn't want her to be alone.

"Where are we going to get flowers from?" Jordan asked.

They all turned to look at Greyson but he shrugged his shoulders he knew nothing about flowers or where to find them.

"Leave that up to me." Jason stated in an excited tone

CHAPTER 30

THE UNEXPECTED FUNERAL

Most funerals are unexpected, yes, the funeral is planned but the deaths are not.

Isabella had no idea where to place herself she wanted to comfort Melanie but she was too scared to face her just yet. She couldn't help with the funeral because she would have no idea what to do. She blames herself for everything that's going on around her even the things that her out of her control.

"Izzy. How's the arm." Lila asked while entering the one of the bedrooms in the ship.

With all that was going on Isabella had nearly forgotten the fact that she had injured her arm, but she was also trying to forget everything that had happened.

"It's not that bad. How's Melanie?" She said while trying to change the subject.

"As well as can be expected." Lila said.

Isabella had always hated phrases like that. It never told her anything it was as if they were trying to keep her in the dark but what was there to hide, Noah was dead. Quickly, Lila left the room she felt like they were all avoiding her she didn't blame them though she already felt guilty about Noah.

"And done!" Jason's half excited voice shouted.

What he could be excited about he's planning a funeral not a wedding Isabella thought.

"What do you think?" Jason asked Brooklyn while showing her the flowers on the table.

Brooklyn had no idea how he was keeping it together every time she thought of him, she felt her heart break.

Tears welled up in Brooklyn's eyes.

"You're psychotic. How are you excited about this? Noah's dead and Melanie and Blake are shutting everyone out. So how are you keeping it all together?" Brooklyn yelled.

He pulled her into a comforting hug. Deep down he wasn't alright but no one around him was alright he just didn't want people to worry about him.

"It's better if I'm busy. Plus, if this funeral is going to help the group somehow say good bye to this young boy I want to help. I know I have to say good bye as well but if I don't focus on that I can bury them feelings."

Dear diary,

My name is Jordan Amulet. I found this under the bed in the captain's cabin. There's nothing much in here but I thought I would give it a shot.

No one is safe we have lived our lives in false safety it was only a matter of time till that shattered. Our lives are like a shard of broken glass sometimes pretty to look at, but you wouldn't want to get too close, or it might cut you. It's also part of something much bigger than any of us even if some of us aren't quite sure about it.

Melanie's locked herself in one of the rooms again I know what it's like to lose her brother I wish I could tell her it will get better but I can't lie to her. She will carry his death with her for as long as she lives.

~~While Blake r~~ I'm not sure what he's doing I've seen him I have even spoken to him but he doesn't seem to even be in the room when any of us are talking to him.

The funeral is at sunset today apparently it was Noah's favourite time of the day I guess that's one thing we have in common.

Stay with me stay with me. Melanie's eyes shot open as she gasped for breath. He's not dead he's not dead. The world disappeared into a blur everything in the room was spinning. Pain wrapped its burning fingers around her throat, killing away the last remnants of her hopeful memories. Her knees felt weak, is this the blink of insanity Melanie thought. Her heart began to pound, every unbearable tear sent memories to her mind memories she longed to forget. She screamed until her lungs were sore. The voices yelled at her while tearing away at her soul her lungs ached as tears broke like glass down her face.

Despite, trying to ignore everyone the second Blake heard Melanie scream he ran into the room and pulled her into a well-needed hug.

Blake knew he couldn't help her but he could hold her while her entire world was collapsing, he knew she will eventually pick up her broken pieces but that was not today. All he could do was to be there for the people it hurt most. No matter how much it affected him he would always put Melanie first from now on.

The sound of the knock on the door echoed throughout the silent room.

"I just wanted to let you know we are ready for you but just take your time." Greyson stated while trying to hide the sobs.

Blake looked down at Melanie he knew she wasn't ready to say goodbye but he also knew she would never have been ready to say goodbye.

As the two walked out onto the main deck the others formed a semi-circle surrounding Noah. Melanie clutched onto Blake as if he was a walking stick, she knew if she let go of him, she would fall.

Jason had placed Noah on a raft that they had pulled together with a type of vine. He was surrounded with lavender coloured roses and white daisies.

"Goodbye buddy we will meet again in another lifetime who knows maybe we will make a difference." Blake chuckled.

Even if they weren't related by blood Blake and Noah were closer than brothers.

His final words were repeating themselves in Isabella's mind he didn't want to die. He wasn't ready to die.

Part Five
Fighting
A
Loosing
Battle

Chapter 31

Remorse, Guilt or Greed...Finding her!

Alexandra felt as if she was counting the minutes to her death, it wouldn't be long till she passed out from the bullet. She felt herself slowly begin to drift off it had only been a matter of hours since Blake had left her tied to a tree. Deep down she knew she deserved it but she at least hoped he would kill her quickly instead of dragging it out.

Horse's hooves began to stomp against the ground, she could hear them getting closer, but she couldn't tell if to jump for joy or to cry. The horse could mean two things, number one a purple trying to leave the country or in her worse case it could be the very same type of people that tried to kill her less than five hours ago.

The sky had already started to get darker the bright never-ending blues had started to fade away into a much richer colour but that was also when the stars would begin to show.

In the end I am my own nightmare Alexandra thought while gradually giving up.

Eventually her eyes locked shut she could tell someone was towering over but she didn't have an ounce of energy to spare.

He carried her into the carriage and carefully placed her on the left side. Her blue-coloured dress with expensive silver sewn into the front of it. But the dress was stained scarlet red most of it was her blood but a few drops of it belonged to the boy she believed to be still alive.

"Why is the princess so far away from home?" The teenager spoke in a threatening tone while spinning a knife between his fingers.

Her eyes opened as if it were the last time, they would ever open.

"Don't." She begged.

His eyes looked up as if he was shocked to have seen her awake. She uncontrollably fiddled with her fingers while trying to keep her distance from the stranger.

His eyes were sending daggers at her but even she had no idea why.

"What do you want with me?" She asked.

For the first time since she had awakened his eyes drifted away from her and looked outside to the bare trees with heavy snow hanging off their skinny arms.

He should've spoken something but he didn't.

POW! One of the wheels had been taken out.

POW! The stranger jumped up and looked at the front of the carriage to see absolutely nothing. No one was there.

POW! Both drivers had been taken out. The horses had run out into the wilderness. They were in the middle of nowhere they were surrounded by forest.

"We have to go now." He demanded.

He grabbed her hand and pulled her out of the carriage. He couldn't tell where the shots had come from. But he knew one thing he wasn't going to wait for another one to be fired. Without even giving Alexandra a second to catch her breath he grabbed her hand again and they both disappeared.

The carriage stood still there was not a single sound everything almost looked dead.

"They're still alive. I won't come back until I have their heads. All of them." A stranger from the side of the road spoke in a deadly voice.

If only they had stayed a matter of seconds, they would've overheard and would've ran for dear life.

But they vanished.

"Who are you?" Alexandra gasped for breath.

The ringing in her ears had reached an unbearable level. It was as if every second she was gasping for breath.

Her head felt as if it were stuck on a rollercoaster and unable to ever get off.

"Can we stop?" She breathed.

Without even having a minute to think about what she had just said she collapsed.

"Again." The stranger rolled his eyes.

Her face glowed a scarlet red colour within seconds he had pulled his water flask out of his bag and placed cold water on her lips they had turned as white as the snow surrounding. Them. He had read somewhere that water will help cool her down.

He carefully placed her next to him if he hadn't checked he would've assumed she was dead.

Chapter 32

The Shadow Murderer

Her eye floated around staring at objects but they went straight back to a complete blur.

"You're okay just breath your vision should come back in a few minutes." A calming voice spoke to Alexandra.

She could only make out a tall shape but all the colour started blending into each other which caused her breathing to increase.

He placed his hand in hers to try calm her down.

"My name is Theo. Theo Hunter.'' He spoke in a soothing tone.

While he talked Alexandra heavily searched her mind, she knew that last name but where had she heard it from. It could only mean danger she was raised in a castle filled with heartless killers. There was only a handful of people who weren't killers but then again, they still answered to the king. They all did.

Hunter. Hunter. Hunter. Her mind wildly repeated the name until she could remember where she had heard it from.

"Blake Hunter. You're his brother aren't you?" She panicked.

It was as if he flipped a switch his eyes turned dark not in colour though she could now only imagine all the horrors he has committed.

"How do you know that name?" He screamed.

Despite him screaming at her and towering over him she didn't even move.

His eyes scanned the floor until they came across the dagger he had dropped before. He grabbed it and pulled it up to her bare neck he then mouthed the words 'If you don't answer me, I will drive this dagger through your neck'.

"I've known him for a while, but he now hates me more than Isabella."

After she finished speaking, they sat in a suffocating silence.

The blues had been told that they both have defied the king not together though but now they have all been notified that they are working together. Whereas the purples know that the two are world class killers. This was the one thing that both sides would ever agree with.

"Why were you attached to a tree when I found you?" He questioned.

"I led a group of purples to safety but instead of staying I left on a horse. At the time I was unaware that Melanie was also on the horse. It was as if my mind had gone completely blank. Despite not thinking straight I knew we were on a suicide mission and I wouldn't have been surprised if they knew it too. So, your brother thought death was a suitable punishment but now the whole entire world is searching for me. Both sides want me dead. If I am found though I hope the guards find me because it will be quicker because the purples are looking for revenge. Revenge is never quick." Alexandra blurted out.

Honestly, Theo knew she had some sort of insane story that had led her to him but his story was just as crazy.

"I defied the Generals orders who also just happens to be my grandad. If you were with Blake then I guess you know Noah about three years ago I threatened to kill him." Theo began to explain how he had come across Alexandra.

"You tried to kill a six-year-old that's low and that's coming from me."

Theo rolled his eyes.

"I regretted that so I waited till they climbed over the wall to call the guards so they had enough time to vanish. They should've stayed where they were. Noah was killed. I watched as a guard shot him. I looked directly into my grandfather's eyes as I shot the guard." He gloated.

It was early morning and neither of them had gotten enough sleep the only time Alexandra had been able to close her eyes was when she was passed out. Theo was too paranoid to even blink. The forest was so silent he could hear his heart beat.

Theo lied a bit it wasn't as extravagant as he described killing the guard destroyed his potential future, but he owed Noah a lot.

"How were you raised I mean we have similar stories but I believe yours could have a full book written about it." Alexandra joked.

"I was trained to become a villain, but I became something worse than they could ever have imagined." He laughed.

"Maybe we are all villains and it just depends on who's telling the story." Alexandra added.

They headed off to hunt, both were starving but they could last a few more hours without food.

The trees stood still; fog was trapped inside the never-ending forest it only lightly revealed some of the tree's roots that were sticking out of the uneven ground. There were a few patches of icy snow but most of the ground was pure grass and thick mud.

Alexandra's shoe kept getting caught in the mud, so she ended up having to take her shoes off and throwing them away. They were covered in mud and had already started to wear away. "We should have found something already. Chances are we shall starve to death before this bloody killer has another chance to shoot at us." Theo spat.

"If you're quiet we might actually catch something." Alexandra scolded.

We still have one flask full of water which could last us a day slightly longer but not long he may be right we will die before the killer finds us Alexandra grimaced.

"Look. Look." Alexandra whispered violently.

The deer stood in between the two tallest trees and lay down. Alexandra was glaring at Theo but he didn't get the message at all instead he just glared back at her. Without giving him a minute to try and think of what she could have meant she grabbed his gun and shot the deer twice.

"I could've done that." Theo screamed.

"Yeah, but you didn't." Alexandra answered in a cheery tone.

The fire was the only thing that lit up the forest everything else looked like it could be a murderer's theme park. Well, there is one murder around, but they haven't been seen for over twenty-four hour's they're waiting till we're vulnerable Theo thought. But we are already vulnerable in fact they could strike this second and we would still be caught off guard Theo added.

"Stop thinking about it." Alexandra demanded.

"No. How do you know they're not staring straight at us?" Theo panicked.

She looked back at the fire to see the part of the deer beginning to cook the flames were dancing around the fire-proof pot. This couldn't have been the first time Theo's thought about running away because he wouldn't have brought all these supplies Alexandra thought intensely.

Theo's eyes darted forward, he tried to tell himself he was imagining it, but he was thrilled that he didn't listen to the voice inside his head. He wasn't wrong there was someone there, but he didn't want to startle Alexandra, he tried to play it off as if he didn't know the murderer was less than five feet in front of them.

Although Theo had a feeling the killer wanted him to know he was there so instead of hesitating he yanked his gun out of his bag and pulled the trigger.

The shadow fell to the floor, but it was still alive. It all happened so quickly that it was only at this moment that

Alexandra had registered what she had just witnessed. The killer had been shot.

Theo dragged the shadow towards the fire while leaving the mask which was the only thing protecting the shadow from them.

Within a blink of an eye, Theo had already pinned the shadow murder to the floor.

"If you don't tell us what your business is here. I will kill you slowly and even more painful than you could ever imagine." Theo threatened.

"You are a psychopath." Alexandra stated.

"I prefer creative love!" Theo shouted.

The mask was painted as black as coal with only little gaps for breathing. You would never have thought that the mask was letting enough air for the murder to breath.

Viciously, Theo placed his left hand over the killer's air holes. Alexandra watched as fear attacked the killer's eyes but they didn't move it was as if they were trying to fight death when it was staring straight at them.

"Tell us who you are." Theo demanded.

Theo turned back to check on Alexandra but he's shouldn't have. Number one rule of kidnapping never turn your back on the person you have kidnapped.

"Alexan-"

The killer had whacked Theo over the head with the burning pan. Theo's body clashed into the floor.

The killer lunged towards her but she dashed out the way. This is not how I am going to die Alexandra repeated in her chaotic mind.

The killer grabbed for Theo's gun but they were too late she had already vanished into the forest for the second time.

This time the killer had to dial the number.

It rang five times till someone answered.

"The girl ran off again but I've got him." The shadow spoke proudly.

Theo was only lightly breathing but not enough to make him look alive.

"I'm pretty sure he's dead though." The shadow added.

The shadows conversation became unbearable for Theo to listen in to but he tried his best to blank it out. His only chance of survival was to run no matter how much pain it caused him.

The only thing that was known about the shadow was that they were one hundred percent a blue. The first mistake the shadow had made was slightly rolling up their sleeve which revealed their mark.

Not a single mark is the same they always look slightly different but Theo didn't get a good enough look to be able to point it out from a crowd.

Patiently, he waited until it was the right moment to jump up and leave but would it ever be the right moment he thought. There is no perfect chance the next time they turn around I will leave Theo decided.

Quickly, Theo jumped up from the muddy ground and sprinted in the same direction as Alexandra had.

It took only second for the killer to start chasing after him but he soon lost them. But how long will it take for them to find him Theo thought.

A mental image replaced, them chaotic thoughts with fear what if they already have found Alexandra Theo imagined.

Chapter 33

Fear isn't a weakness it's a strength.

Like a giant fist the waves rose and slammed into the shore, savage and fierce. The cloudless vibrant sky was hiding the painful truth which is reality.

It wouldn't be long till they all had to get back onto the boat. It was as if all the hope and joy in their lives had been sucked out and to never return.

Rage violently ran through Melanie's body. Only one thing was on her mind and it wasn't being friendly her body was emotionally and physically exhausted she didn't know if she wanted to scream or cry, but she was unable to do either.

Motivation had completely left Blake's mind it was as if his mind were a blank canvas with nothing to be painted.

Fear was the only thing preoccupying Lila's mind it was as if she had finally woken up from her fantasy dream.

They had all had a wake-up call nothing is going to change unless they change it.

Hopeless was the only thing that could have described Brooklyn at this moment in time she had lost everything even the people who were still breathing it was as if they were gone.

"I think he found peace." Brooklyn spoke while breaking their deafening thoughts.

Greyson had practically buried himself in the burning sand but he was the only one who hadn't given up not yet any way.

"I think he would want us to fight." Greyson joked.

"We should fight." Melanie agreed.

Blake and Greyson both pulled the same concerned face they both thought the same thing this was clearly a suicide mission.

"I was joking." Greyson clarified.

The first smile Melanie had pulled drifted away with in seconds.

"What's the point in surviving if we never actually get to live our lives?" Melanie cried.

"She's right. I don't want to spend every second of my life running from shadows." Jordan agreed.

Blake placed in hand on his head and took a deep breath.

"By this point we have all almost died more times than I can count, and now we have lost Noah. SO yeah, I agree with her." Jason boomed.

Isabella looked up from the sand to see Blake's furious face.

"Blake calm down. There not wrong hundreds of men, women and children are tortured and killed every day. If we can even make a small difference to that I don't get why we wouldn't help." Isabella stated.

It was five against two but luckily Greyson and Blake agreed no matter how much they knew this was going to be their downfall. They still agreed.

Greyson knew what they were all doing pressuring themselves with all these jobs they want to get done just to hide the pain that has been created inside of them. Despite, the fact he knew they were using this as a coping mechanism he didn't stop them or tell them about it, but then again, he was never one to talk about feelings.

The brutal wind hit them in the face when they were standing on the deck of the boat.

"I am sorry we all voted against your decision." Lila apologised while walking towards the steering wheel.

"Oh, it's fine Lila. It's about what you believe in not what I believe in." Greyson sighed.

"Yes, but what I believe in could end up getting us all killed or worse tortured." Lila added.

They all believed that death was better than being tortured and even worse was being tortured to death. Jason feared both deeply he always believed he was born in the worst universe his two biggest fears are inevitable.

"One day when this is all over will you teach me how to steer this thing." Lila asked.

Greyson nodded but he knew they would both be long gone before this is all over.

Brooklyn walked onto the main deck and chuckled as she watched Greyson and Lila talk.

"I bet you twenty-five gold coins they end up together and have a family." Brooklyn laughed.

"Okay I bet against it." Jason joked.

The only thing that was preoccupying Blake's mind was the scarce food supply. It was running out quicker than he could have imagined.

"Shit training boats." Lila screamed.

Those three words created everyone on the boat to run to the main deck.

"Okay everyone split half go on the left side half go on the right and hold on." Greyson yelled.

The ship moved as fast as it could but Greyson was unsure how long it could keep going like this till it stopped working.

Waves were coming over the top of the boat and drenching everyone. The sky turned to a savage grey and rain started bouncing off the wooden deck.

The boats were catching up with them.

"IF I GET PAST THOSE ROCKS, I HAVE A HIGH CHANCE OF GETTING PAST THEM!" Greyson shouted.

The restless storm battered the ship.

"WAIT DID YOU SAY ROCKS!" Jason screamed.

The dress Brooklyn was wearing was half torn through the middle and soaked through.

Jason's gripped onto the side of the boat while Blake was laughing.

"HOLD ON." Greyson yelled.

The boat had tipped backwards but Greyson wasn't planning on falling to his death not today not ever. I am going to have a life with the one I love and a million adopted children and I am going to name one after Noah Greyson motivated himself.

Melanie was barely hanging onto the boat but Jordan kept tight of hold of her.

"IT WILL BE OVER IN THIRTY SECONDS WE WILL HAVE LOST THEM BY THEN." Greyson shouted.

Greyson wasn't wrong they lost both ships but the storm was sill chaotic and terrorizing. The ship was violently shaking and terrifying everyone who was on. The waves were savagely taking over the boat.

It took almost two hours for them to escape the storm. After the storm, the ocean sat still and calm, reflecting the sky like a mirror.

"It's way too cold." Lila shivered.

Melanie ran up to the top deck where Greyson was steering the ship she dived into his arms and hugged him.

"Woah, what's this for? You are soaking wet." Greyson chuckled.

"I know I just thought you were too dry up here. Thank you for not steering us straight into rocks." Melanie shouted while walking back into one of the rooms.

But as soon as she locked herself into the room tears formed in her eyes. Sadness crushed her with the overwhelming force of a tidal wave and she drowned in its embrace.

"Noah come back!" Melanie screamed into her pillow.

Blake stood still outside of her room. His heart was breaking at her cries he knew there was nothing he could do to stop the pain she's going through.

"Do you really think we will make it out of this alive?" Isabella asked Brooklyn.

Brooklyn had wrapped herself around about five towels but it wasn't warming her up at all her fingers and toes had gone numb.

"No, I think I am going to die of hyperthermia." Brooklyn stated.

Isabella chuckled at the fact that Brooklyn had placed a towel around her head.

"I wasn't joking." Brooklyn said.

Isabella walked back out of the room and back onto the deck the sea air was fresh and for the first time in a while the waves were calm and drifting straight past the ship.

Chapter 34

What else can possibly go wrong?

Greyson sat watching the sun slowly set. It was as if the sky were a faucet, steadily draining the warm colours into a vacuum of an empty void.

Blake summoned everyone into the captain's cabin. None of them knew why they were not even Melanie the only person who Blake talked to.

"I have a plan." Blake stated dramatically.

Hope lit up inside Isabella's eyes but she wasn't the only one for the first time since Noah was killed Melanie was hopeful that she might have a chance of a normal life.

"What's the plan, boss." Greyson joked.

"Every year the King and Queen hold a ball for all the most accomplished guards and their families. We're going to get in. How you may ask? Me, Isabella, and

Melanie are going to be the ones inside the ball. Greyson and Jason you two will be our eyes and ears I want you to know everything that is going on and all times. Lila and Brooklyn you two must find disguises for us to wear so no one will recognise us. Especially Melanie since her farther shall be there."

"What's the aim of this?" Melanie asked.

"To find out all their plans and we will destroy them." Blake announced.

Greyson thought deeply about Blake's plans it wasn't an air tight plan because there we so many ways they could be killed.

"See as much as I love that plan, I have a better one. You still go to the ball and all that stuff but why don't we blow it therefore we find out their plans and kill a lot of our main targets. Unless that would affect Melanie as her father is inside." Greyson considered.

All of them turned to look at Melanie they all expected her to disagree with the plan due to her father being there but Blake already knew what she would say.

"I hope he rots in hell." Melanie commented.

"One problem though do any of you know how to make or activate a bomb." Jason questioned.

They all shook their head no.

"I thought so." Jason murmured.

"I know someone but we would have to break her out of the guard if we wanted her to help us." Isabella announced.

"I am sorry but we don't have enough to time to plan and break someone out of the guard if we did that now we would be heading to our deaths." Blake apologized.

"We have three and a half months to plan. The way I look at it they are both suicide missions but we all agreed that we are going to make a difference or at least try." Lila stated.

The day ended swiftly but none of them really knew where to put themselves other than Greyson who was steering the boat.

"I can take over if you want." Jason offered.

"No, it's fine." Greyson politely declined.

Jason walked over to the steering wheel.

"You haven't slept in three days go and get some rest now." Jason demanded.

Luckily, Greyson agreed and slept for the first time in seventy-two hours. Honestly, Jason didn't really want to take the wheel but he had nothing else to do.

"Blake, do you think this plan will work." Brooklyn asked him.

"Greyson and I made it. Of course, it will work." Blake spoke in a cheerful tone.

"Excuse me." Blake added.

Brooklyn knew that they weren't one hundred percent sure it would work but at this moment she didn't care.

Morning came quite quickly to be honest they were all quite sure that Jason would have crashed the ship.

"You're steering us the wrong way north is that way!" Greyson boomed.

"NO THAT IS SOUTH YOU IDIOT." Jason yelled back at him.

Blake stumbled up the stairs to the main deck due to Greyson and Jason arguing.

"You both need marriage counselling. Jason go help Brooklyn. NOW. Greyson try not to crash the ship." Blake demanded.

Without even a word of debate Jason hurried down the stairs and into Brooklyn's room. A smirk formed on Blake's face.

"Don't even." Greyson responded.

"I wasn't going to say anything but now that you think I was going to say something I don't need to say it." Blake vaguely explained.

Greyson just looked at him with a face full of confusion but he didn't answer with anything.

Melanie had locked herself in her room again as usual he waited outside until she called for him. The second she did he rushed in and comforted her. It was as if he had locked all his thoughts and feelings in a locked chest deep inside of him and he didn't plan on opening it anytime soon.

"He's in a better place." Blake reassured her but he wasn't exactly sure what happened after death but then again who is.

Nothing can be worse than this he thought.

"Blake, we have a problem." Brooklyn spoke in a concerning tone.

What else can go wrong Blake thought as he left Melanie's room? Brooklyn guided him into the captain's cabin where Jason was watching the waves go past the boat.

"We have run out of food rations and water is very quickly running out." Jason stated.

"Lila and I already had to go to land anyway so I guess food is just add on job right 'boss'." Brooklyn announced.

Blake closed his eyes tight shut nothing else can possibly go wrong he repeated.

Lila dashed down the broken wooden steps and into the captain's cabin.

"Boss, we have a problem." Lila belted.

 As soon as she had finished the sentence, she sprinted straight out of the room causing everyone to follow her. They followed her to the top deck where Greyson was standing over Jordan.

"Shit. What happened?" Blake yelled.

 They were all in too much shock but Blake's shouting caused Melanie and Isabella to rush out of their rooms.

"Go back inside Melanie you too Isabella." Blake demanded.

Although his shouting did frighten them, they stayed on the main deck. Greyson was trying to speak but his words came out slurred and inaudible.

"She's losing too much blood. I need t-" Isabella spoke.

Blake placed his hand on her arm to try stop her.

"You've been through too much these past days you aren't in the right head space."

Isabella cut him off before he could say anything else she kneeled next to Jordan and kept pressure on her leg to try keep the blood inside of her.

"Everyone go inside except Jason." She demanded.

Shock formed on Blake's face but surprisingly he followed her orders which was unlike him but if it saved Jordan he didn't care.

Impatiently, they all sat inside the captain's cabin except Blake who was pacing as if there was no tomorrow.

"Blake could you just-" Greyson whispered.

"Can I just what sit quietly and not worry about her. No, I just can't for all we know she could already be dead. I still don't know how it happened." Blake hissed.

The only emotions they had ever been taught was fear and sadness they should be used to it by now but they all wondered if they would ever get used to this feeling.

Isabella knocked on the door and slowly walked in but it wasn't a smile that was on her face. Quite the opposite her emotions looked fairly like when she watched Noah die.

Brooklyn felt her heart drop as she saw the expression that was painted on Isabella's face.

"She's alive but we don't know if she will be able to walk again." Isabella whispered. She then added "We have to get to land so one of us can go steal some pain killers."

None of them knew how to react, they would have understood how to react if she had died but she wasn't but they all knew she was better off dead with only one leg.

"She won't survive." Blake muttered.

They were all thinking it but none of them wanted to say it.

"Don't say that Blake she is fine." Isabella cried.

Melanie walked into the room still unaware of what had happened.

"What's going on?" She shouted.

Their heads all turned to her the girl who had lost her brother less than three days ago none of them knew how to explain what had happened.

"A small boat passed and they must've known where to find us and they shot at me but Jordan dived in the way. She got shot in her leg. Isabella, thinks Jordan may not be able to walk again." Greyson admitted.

"She won't be able to walk. She won't be able to run." Melanie sobbed.

They all knew if you weren't a blue and you couldn't walk your chances of survival were zero. Even if a guard found her, they wouldn't take her to The Gaol' they would just kill her.

None of them knew how to comfort one another and the moment Jordan woke up none of them knew what to say or how to act.

"What does this mean?" Lila asked the rest of the group.

Isabella and Brooklyn both shrugged their shoulders where the rest stayed silent.

"This. This means war." Blake announced.

Light lit up in their eyes they were done dismissing the war that was about to be everywhere. They all knew someone was going to demand war but not even one of them thought it would be Blake.

"Okay 'Boss'" Greyson cheered.

"Stop calling me boss that ends now." Blake demanded while leaving the room.

"Okay 'Boss'" They all shouted in unison.

Blake rolled his eyes but as soon as he knocked on Jordan's door his expression changed immediately. He walked into her room with his head facing the ground.

"How are you feeling?" He questioned.

"It kills but the medication has taken an edge off it but not for long. You can look at me you know." She muttered.

His eyes lifted from the ground. His heart broke into pieces the second he looked at her. Guilt had consumed him like a wildfire, he could feel it burning through his mind no matter how much he tried to reassure himself that he couldn't have stopped this, but he knew he was lying to himself. He could have stopped this.

"This wasn't your fault." She sobbed while trying to stop the tears. "I am useless now aren't I? You're just going to throw me to the wolves."

He knew they had a complicated relationship but he never wanted her to feel like this. In fact, he couldn't imagine his life without her annoying little inputs on life.

"I would never do that to you. You're definitely not useless Jordan." He revealed.

No matter how much she wanted to be happy by the fact that he cared about her she wasn't happy at all. Deep down she knew the second they stepped into war she would be their first target.

CHAPTER 35

THE NEW PLAN

Carefully, Blake carried Jordan into the captain's cabin which may as well be called the meeting room since everything is talked about in that room. Everyone was sitting around the table except Greyson who was steering the ship but half way through him and Jason would switch places.

"Isabella you are now our official medic. I know some of you are wondering how we are going pull it off. We are going to split into three groups. One group will go brake Willow out of The Gaol' and group two will go to the main town and steal medical supplies and the three disguises for me, Isabella, and Melanie. Group three will stay here and make sure we don't get caught you will be our eyes and ears for group one and two." Blake began.

"Jason take over for me." Greyson shouted from top deck.

They could leave the ship for longer than two seconds but none of them wanted to chance it. If they were going to die it wasn't going to be because someone wasn't steering the ship.

Blake recapped himself a bit but Greyson had already listened into most of it. Surprisingly, Greyson had unusual heightened senses.

"Group one will be Me, Greyson, and Isabella. Group two will be Brooklyn, Melanie, and Lila. Group three will be Jason and Jordan." Blake continued.

Lila stared blankly at the people who were standing in front of her she could tell they were talking hut didn't understand any of the words that were coming out of their mouth. It was as if they were talking in language that only they understood.

"LILA!" Greyson shouted trying to get her attention.

Despite, him yelling at her she didn't move a muscle she just stared into thin air. At this moment it was as if she wasn't even in the same room as them. Isabella walked up to her and stared into Lila's eyes but the girl didn't move.

Her hands started to violently shake but Lila wasn't even aware of anything. It was as if she was nothing but at the same time everything.

"Lila if you can hear me squeeze my hand." Isabella advised.

But there was no response she didn't move for only a moment it looked like she stopped breathing all together. Neither of them understood how she was still standing.

"HELP!" Lila screamed.

Blake glanced at Isabella who looked like a mixture of terrified and confused.

"She will be alright." He whispered.

Although, he didn't believe a word he was saying he knew it wouldn't be long till one of them acted like this. Eventually, Lila came around but she was still unaware of everything that had happened.

Days passed without anyone mentioning Lila's episode it was also the last time Blake and Isabella spoke.

"Izzy." Jason yelled from outside of her room.

She glanced outside her door with a face filled with confusion.

"Why are you calling me Izzy?" Isabella questioned.

Jason walked into the meeting room without saying another word, she followed him Blake and Greyson were in the room facing the window but Jason left without another word. His running echoed throughout the ship to go steer the boat Isabella thought.

"Why am I here?" Isabella asked them both.

But neither of the answered they just turned around and stared at her.

"Do these look realistic?" Blake inquired while they both slowly rolled their left sleeve up to reveal a blue patterned mark, they both had one but they looked totally different.

"Realistic enough to make me have a heart attack!" She screamed.

They both looked at her and laughed.

"They are part of our disguise. We have over forty of them." Greyson exclaimed.

"Is there any chance you could get Group two to steal more than just three outfits." Isabella laughed.

"Why do you think they leave first? We will wait till they come back then we will set off to The Gaol.' We will be going in disguised as Guards. Hopefully, they won't recognise us." Blake explained.

"Greyson killed every one last time we were there. If anyone recognises us, I will pay you both ten gold coins." Isabella joked.

Meanwhile, Jordan couldn't stand the feeling of being a burden to the rest of the group. None of them acted normal around her she could tell they were all walking one eggshell around her. She felt even more embarrassed when Blake and Jason had to either carry or help her walk to places.

Lucky enough for her the bathroom was just outside her room. Although, she still struggled to get there but she wasn't going to complain.

"Are you feeling better?" Brooklyn asked.

Jordan's head tilted towards the door. Am I feeling better this question haunts me more than my missing leg Jordan thought continuously? Jordan wanted to break down without affecting anyone she just didn't know how to deal with it. The pain killers weren't seeming to help it was as if her leg was being cut off at every moment

On the odd time that she would even get the slightest ounce of sleep she would wake up screaming causing either Blake or Jason to run in like there was no tomorrow. It took them several times to reassure her that her leg was still there. Jordan felt as if everyone was talking about how weak she was they didn't have to be saying the words or thinking the thoughts if she believed it, it would haunt her for the rest of the day.

"Yeah. I am fine." Jordan reassured her.

Brooklyn could tell she was lying but she also knew Jordan was very similar to Blake he never really expressed his feelings.

"Do you remember the time where Jason just up and decided that he was moving in with us!" Brooklyn laughed.

Jordan laughed but her also remembering that being one of the worst experiences of her life not even halfway through the first day Brooklyn had been kidnapped.

"Yeah!" Jordan joked.

Group two was set to leave the next morning.

For Lila fear felt like a thousand needles breaking through her skin. Whereas, Melanie on the other hand was more excited to start doing something. Brooklyn just wanted to get off the boat she had been sea sick more time than she could count.

The next day couldn't have come quick enough. They arrived at the docks at around six in the morning. The only two people who were awake were Jason and Jordan who were siting at the top deck.

Blake had prepared everyone for the questions they might get but no one knew who they were. Other than Jason who was told to hide whenever someone came close to the boat.

The night before Blake had given everyone their replacement marks that covered their purple mark perfectly. It was too early in the morning for anyone else to be in the docks. Although within a few hours this place will be more packed than the main market.

Chapter 36

Group 2 gone wrong

"WAKE UP!" Jason belted through the speakers.

Jason's screaming caused everyone to wake up and caused Blake and Greyson to run onto the main deck like there was no tomorrow.

"What was my first rule that I made very clear last night?" Blake shouted at Jason.

Jason was laughing hysterically because he could see Blake's vein going to pop out of his head.

"Don't create a scene." Jason joked.

Blake furiously ran up the stairs with Greyson. He's going to kill me Jason mouthed to Jordan.

"And what did you do?" Blake demanded.

Jason looked back at Jordan who was trying to stop herself from laughing but they both knew that wasn't going to last long.

"I created a scene." Jason admitted.

The second Blake walked back down the stairs Jason and Greyson started laughing. Whereas Jordan never stopped.

Everyone began to gather in the captain's cabin none of group two knew their way around the town. Blake placed a humongous map on the table while he pointed at all the places, he wanted them to rob.

"And none of you think we're going to get lost." Melanie announced.

They all looked up from the map and nodded.

"Good to know." Melanie added.

Blake wanted them to rob several places to the point where it worried Melanie. There was a higher chance of this plan failing than succeeding but she couldn't back out now.

"Here is forty gold coins in case you're uncomfortable with robbing one of the stores but only one." Blake stated.

"I guess we're ready." Brooklyn announced

Ready as I will ever be Lila thought. They all walked up to the main deck Blake helped them off the boat and watched them leave. He would never admit this to anyone but he felt his heart stop as they left and deep down, he knew it wouldn't return till they arrived safely back.

The old cobbled paths led to the main square which looked as if it could've been made in the 19th century. The main centre was filled with picnic areas but none of the shops were in sight.

"Where are the shops?" Melanie whispered to Brooklyn.

Brooklyn shrugged her shoulders. While they both watched Lila walk up to one of the guards that were standing against one of the walls.

"Excuse me, sir. I and my wife and daughter are traveling and we have been trying to find the shops around here but we can't find them. Could you tell us where they are?" Lila asked the killer.

Melanie and Brooklyn's hearts dropped as he had taken his glove off his hand.

"If you keep walking up to the top you will reach the main shopping area." The guard spoke.

Brooklyn sighed in relief as Lila walked back up to them. When they walked out of the main square none of them looked back. Their hearts were beating too fast to walk up a hill so they stopped at sat against one of the walls outside the square.

"Your wife and child." Brooklyn laughed.

"Shut up, I panicked." Lila said while jokingly punching Brooklyn in the arm.

"Are we going to get going 'mom" Melanie joked.

Lila shot a death stare at Melanie which automatically caused her to keep her mouth shut.

The hill caused them to start losing their breath. Brooklyn placed the backpack on the floor and felt herself collapse to the ground.

"I think this just proves how little exercise we do." Lila breathlessly stated.

"No, I do exercise." Brooklyn reassured her.

Melanie picked the backup up from the floor while saying "Running for life doesn't count."

"No, it's just a hobby." Brooklyn admitted.

The shopping centre was packed and guards stood at every corner which made this even more impossible, they were randomly checking people but as soon something suspicious happens they will be on high alert.

"We should go to Hanna's dressmaking shop first." Lila whispered.

The shop was the closest one to them. All the shops matched the town with their old-fashioned look on the outside. But inside the shop was another world. The dress shop looked triple the size from the inside and each section was carefully chosen.

Every section was colour coordinated everything looked magnificent. Melanie had always dreamed of opening a clothes shop with her brother but she knew that was an impossible dream, especially now.

Tears formed in her eyes but she quickly turned around and rubbed her eyes dry.

"Ok Melanie go look for dresses that you think would suit the occasion. Melanie try and find something that makes you look cute and innocent. But not too innocent keep in mind your family are a bunch of murderers." Lila mumbled to Melanie.

Brooklyn and Lila tried to find something that would suit Isabella.

"How does this look?" Melanie said while walking up to them.

Her dress looked stunning it suited her perfectly the dress had a long light blue skirt with a beautiful white top with pearl bead sewn into it to look like snowflakes.

"You look amazing." Lila exclaimed while hugging Melanie.

Brooklyn chuckled and her eyes lit up as she had found the perfect dress for Isabella.

"How about this for Izzy." She excitedly whispered.

 Melanie walked back into the changing room and stuffed the dresses is one of the backpacks. If the tables were turned she would not be stealing but this is what her life had come to.

They didn't know how long it would be till the guards were alerted that there was a thief in the town but they all knew when that did happen, they would automatically assume it was a purple.

"Next shop a normal clothes shop. Just put anything in the basket then we are going to run out and into the pharmacy and buy the medical supplies we need. Then we get the hell out of here." Brooklyn muttered with a straight face.

The only reason they could get away with this was because the town was overflowing with people. On the way in Melanie read in her mind a sign that read all thieves will be prosecuted it also read no skulls allowed funny enough she was both, but she walked in like she owned the place and run out of it like she wanted nothing to do with it in less than ten minutes.

The suits section was very limited most killers would have gotten theirs weeks ago, so Lila just picked one out that she thought Blake might like.

Whereas Melanie and Brooklyn were just filling their baskets with anything they found. They were sick of wearing ragged and soaked clothes but no matter how much stuff they stole they all knew it wouldn't last more than two months.

"The thieves are over there." The old women said while pointing at Melanie and Brooklyn but not Lila.

"Shit." Melanie muttered.

Brooklyn was still unaware of what Melanie and Brooklyn had overheard. Lila grabbed a hold of Melanie and they both ran out of the shop and into the pharmacy while trying not to create an even bigger scene but that was inevitable.

"Brooklyn." Lila hissed.

It was as if Brooklyn was in a world of her own imagination but the moment, she had gotten released from that world was the moment the guard had placed in her cuffs and walked her out of the shop.

"Melanie, we have to go now." Lila mumbled.

It was as if her feet were glued to the floor and her breathing had increased.

Lila ran out of the pharmacy and blended into the crowed but for Brooklyn she stood out. As soon as Brooklyn caught vision of her, she mouthed the words 'Tell them what they want to know. But keep certain things quiet. We will get you out.'

Brooklyn screamed as she was took to the floor her purple skull had already started to show so they would know everything by sunrise. Brooklyn's screams caused tears to form in Lila's eye. But Lila stayed and watched her half-dead carried into a van. She was going to be sent back to a place she had fought so hard to get out of.

The van drove off with deafening sirens blaring off as it drove away.

It was as if Lila had flipped a switch which turned her emotions off as she walked back to the pharmacy. She spent all forty gold coins on medical supplies that was definitely needed.

"Let's go Mel." Lila mumbled under her breath.

Lila placed her arm around Melanie's they weren't physically injured but they felt it more than ever. It was as if their life was torn into two every single day of their lives.

"How will we tell them? We did nothing we should have done something, right." Melanie sobbed.

People were starting to stare but Lila didn't know what to do she couldn't draw more attention to herself.

"I don't care how much you cry you're not getting another necklace." Lila yelled while glancing at the necklace shop.

They all stopped staring most people are used to parents shouting at their children for things like that. As soon as they got to the cobbled hill Lila apologized for screaming at her but Melanie understood why.

"I think we are going to have to tell them the second we get there so if you want to walk around for half an hour we can." Lila mumbled.

Melanie nodded. They walked around the lake for a little while.

Meanwhile back at the boat Blake and Greyson were slowly losing their minds.

"They should be back by now, right." Blake asked Greyson.

Jordan was lying in the middle of the deck with Jason they couldn't help but laugh at how bad Blake was going on that they had only been gone an hour.

"Blake, you asked me this question less than three minutes ago. Like I said before it is Brooklyn the girl who gets sea sick with just thinking about a boat believe me they will be taking their time?" Greyson yelled.

Jordan hopped back to the room she was practically living in by this time.

Every single time she pulled a fake smile she could feel a burning pain in her heart which was the only thing keeping her from believing her own lie. I am worthless she repeated in her mind no matter how many people told her she was worth something she would always think they were lying no matter how much good they talked about her.

"Is Blake still going on about them?" Isabella questioned while standing at the top deck.

"Yes." Greyson shouted back up at her.

"I think I can see them but I am not sure." Isabella added.

Blake dashed up the stairs as if his life depended on it but when we reached the top his heart shattered.

"Where's Brooklyn." He panicked.

Blake shouting that caused Jason to panic but instead of pacing around like a mad man he ran to where he could see Lila and Melanie. But as soon as Jason reached them, they all knew by his reaction it was terrible news.

Chapter 37

Gone Again

"She was caught." Jason sobbed.

Greyson rushed over towards Melanie and Lila to help them back onto the boat.

"We need to leave. Now!" Lila yelled.

As Greyson prepared the ship for another long journey, Blake prepared the rest of the crew for what was about to happen. But as Greyson looked down at the docks, he saw a flock of guards heading there way.

"Blake!" He warned.

Blake looked straight up at Greyson who looked terrified it took Blake a few seconds to understand what Greyson was warning him about.

"Lila, Mel go inside the meeting room. Now." He rushed.

For once they didn't defy his orders but they also knew something was about to happen and neither of them were eager to find out what.

"Blake what's going on?" Isabella asked with a fake smile painted on her face.

"Just smile on follow my lead." Blake smiled.

Greyson jumped down from the top and walked next to Blake who looked as if he was going to pass out at any moment.

Jason and Isabella also stayed above deck but Jason was having a difficult time dealing with his emotions about Brooklyn.

"This boat is very similar to the boat that was stolen at the king's docks not even a matter of weeks ago." One of the guards stated.

It was as if their hearts skipped a beat.

"I wouldn't know anything about that I have been traveling with my wife and my two good friends." Blake admitted in a fake accent while placing an arm around Isabella.

"They recognised me." Jason muttered to Greyson while trying not to bring to much attention to himself.

Greyson made eye contact with one of the guards he tried to smile but it was as if every muscle his body declined that request.

"Names?" The tall guard 'politely' requested.

"Of course, my name is Aaron Grey and this is my husband Jax Grey, and my closet friends are Aurora Blake and Felix Blake." Jason exclaimed while revealing his blue mark.

"Sorry for the inconvenience. It won't happen again." The Guard apologized.

"Yeah, it better not." Greyson muttered as the guards slowly walked away.

It was as if their hearts started beating again the minute the guards were out of sight. Lila and Melanie dashed out of Jordan's room and onto the main deck.

"What happened?" Melanie rushed.

Jason laid in the middle of the floor and kept his eyes shut tight the next time he opened them the boat was moving and Jordan was lying next to him.

"She will be alright. We will get her back safe." Jordan comforted him.

But no number of words would make him believe Brooklyn was safe until he saw her with his own eyes.

A wave from the ocean rose and crashed like the sun retreating behind a cloud.

"It's beautiful isn't it?" Blake said to Isabella.

The ocean is like a vast mirror reflecting all the horrors and beauties in the world.

"I guess, although I could never imagine missing the sound of Brooklyn throwing up." Isabella remembered.

Everyone's plans and thoughts had changed since Brooklyn was kidnapped especially Jordan's and Jason's but they tried to hide it but they weren't doing a good enough job of it.

Chapter 38

Freedom Calling

The Guard had changed dramatically since Brooklyn was last trapped in there. Plus, there was about double the amount of blood on cobbled floor by the time they had left.

Violently, they dragged her into a blinding white room that was over double the size of the prison cells. The marbled door opened and the figure slammed it behind them.

"Brooklyn Adrianna Scott." The figure stated into a recording machine.

Brooklyn's eye lids seemed to get heavier by the second it was now a fight to keep them open but she knew it was a fight she was bound to lose. Her heart was beating loud enough for her to hear it. It was as if it were a drum roll to death, a drum roll that she was not ready for.

The figure walked up to her with a needle. Brooklyn tried to run but every cell in her body was screaming at her to stay still. Her vision had gone blurry it was as if the only thing in this world was colours, no emotions no nothing.

The only thing she could make out was the figure's shadow.

"Wha- do y- want wit- me." Brooklyn stuttered.

The figure placed an ice-cold gloved hand on top of Brooklyn's forehead.

"You are the key to our safety." The figure laughed only moments before Brooklyn blacked out.

The Guard wasn't the only thing that had changed. There was no space left inside it every single cell was filled with two or more innocent people.

Suddenly, a stranger abruptly shook Brooklyn awake.

"Get up now." The woman rushed while helping Brooklyn to her feet.

A loud echoing siren blasted throughout the guard, which caused all of the prisoners to stand up. It was as if their minds were being controlled by the guards.

About two dozen guards flooded The Gaol's' corridors the prisoners faces became even more fearful. The doors of the cells slowly creaked open. A guard stood outside of every cell until the doors opened fully.

Each guard marched into the cell and grabbed a prisoner in Brooklyn's cell it was the woman who had woken her. Helplessly, Brooklyn watched as the old women was dragged away along with around thirty others.

"Where are you taking them?" Brooklyn yelled.

The guards only ignored her and marched back out the same way they entered.

"Where are they taking them?" Brooklyn asked the girl who had hidden herself into the corner.

"No one knows but I can tell you it's not pretty." The girl answered.

Cries and screams filled the cells but that was the last encounter they had with the guards that day. The guard smelt of blood and death and it left a strong taste in their mouths but most of them had gotten used to it by now.

At the same time, every day they were given a piece of stale dry piece of bread with and a small cup of water. On odd days they would add a tiny bit of butter, although those days were rarer than finding gold.

"Who are you if you don't mind me asking?" Brooklyn spoke in a hushed tone.

The girl opened her warm yellow eyes and stared straight through Brooklyn at the guard who was walking past the cells. But the girl didn't say a word it was as if she wasn't even there.

Chapter 39

Could I be the Shadow?

The sun rose quite quickly that morning. Theo had spent all night searching for Alexandra, but she was nowhere to be seen it was as if she had disappeared off earth. Even though, they didn't get along he needed to find her before the shadow killer did or before the killer found him.

Theo hadn't found anything else too suspicious since his last visit with the shadow killer. Even though it was late morning the forest still had an eerie feeling about it.

An evergreen carpet covered the entire forest floor, perfuming the clearing with a pungent yet sweet scent. The overgrown trees blocked out the light of the sun.

The endless forest was an unbelievable temperature, by now he knew he wasn't going to find Alexandra in this jungle maze.

There was a high chance that she had been taken or worse she just up and left. He wouldn't blame her though the last time she saw him he looked pretty dead.

For hours he searched but there was no trace of her left it was at this moment where he eventually started to doubt his own conscious. Did I ever even see the princess, maybe she doesn't even exist his thoughts escalated up to the point where he felt unsafe in his own mind. When finally got himself to admit that she was with him he began to think something so dark and treacherous. Am I the killer it would make sense he thought but there were so many things happening that he couldn't keep up with the thoughts in his own head.

The forest was slowly driving him to insanity he had to leave at that moment in time he couldn't tell what was fiction and what was reality.

The crumbling road looked like it hadn't been used in years but the odd few horses did pass and every time that happened, he would jump over one of the walls and cower behind it.

The ringing sound inside his head was getting louder and louder as if he was getting closer to something he didn't want to find, but he wasn't wrong the thing not too far ahead would shock him to his very core. Luckily enough for him his unstable self-conscious steered him in another direction still not a good direction to walk in but he followed it anyway. His thoughts were like jumbled pieces of a jigsaw that were impossible to piece together.

A trail of scarlet read blood formed in the middle of the road he didn't know whether to follow it or steer clear of it. Fighting against his natural broken instincts he followed it back into the forest. One of the trees it was written in the same scarlet blood 'I know your secret.' To this day he still doesn't know if what he saw was real or his imagination.

It was as if the fear was keeping him hostage in his own self-conscious. For a quick moment he shut his eyes tight and imagined something happy. Although when he opened his eyes, it only got worse this time he was covered in the blood and the sign was smudged. Instead of reopening his eyes for a second time he kept them shut.

Chapter 40

A war is brewing

Everyone on the ship soon became quite irritated. None of them could stand in the same room as one another for longer than five minutes.

"I say we go save Brooklyn now." Jason yelled.

The rest of them were used to Blake and Jason arguing at this time of day. It had been over three weeks since Brooklyn had been taken. They still were going to break Brooklyn and Willow out of The Gaol' but the planning was slow and they were already way too far behind schedule.

"Are you the one breaking into the most heavily guarded place in the world? No so you don't get a say when we leave!" Blake belted.

Isabella was standing at the top of the boat while Greyson eagerly tried to teach her how to steer a boat but her mind was elsewhere. She felt stuck

Unlike everyone else she had been trapped in The Gaol' for a high percentage of her life whereas some of the group only stayed there for a matter of months. She wasn't ready to go back there but she didn't think she would ever be ready to witness the horrors of the guard.

"Promise me one thing." Isabella started. Greyson looked up at her. "You won't let us get stuck there again."

Greyson watched as tears started to form in Isabella's eyes within seconds he jumped up and hugged her.

"I promise, no one will get left behind." Greyson whispered.

Jason and Blake had finally calmed down again and hopefully for the last time, but all knew that wasn't true there would be a new argument tomorrow.

"Greyson get the ship ready." Blake began. Greyson and Isabella both turned around with a confused face. "Where going to break Brooklyn out."

Jason cheered. Funny he was cheering at this moment but in about a week he will regret that.

Lila felt her body stop as she used the railing to hold her up. Sweat dripping off her head. Her heart seemed to beat louder than any drum and struck faster than lightning.

"Izzy help me." Brooklyn cried in desperation.

Within a second Brooklyn's desperation heightened and pure fear took over. "THEY KNOW. THEY KNOW. THEY know…" Brooklyn screamed.

Lila stayed glued to the spot terrified at the thought that this could be the reality Brooklyn suffered. A shadowed hand wrapped around Lila's throat causing all the air to erupt from her lungs. She kicked and screamed but all of Lila's attempts to run vanished. The shadow dropped Lila onto the ground she jumped up and lunged forward. She reached out in attempt to grab the shadow but she fell straight through it and ended up right where she began. Theo Hunter appeared at her feet, his face covered in cuts and bruises, his words barely audible but she could sense his pain.

"Things aren't always as they seem." Theo whispered.

She reached out her hand to aid him but he too disappeared into the emptiness.

"Blake." Lila cried. "Jason." "Greyson." "Jordan."

"Anybody."

"Please please get me out of here. Get me out. Get me out."

Nothing was real in this twisted reality. Nothing. That's what haunted her she knew nothing for all she knew this could very much be true but she refused to let that take over her mind. Lila curled into the darkness blending into the deafening screams and endless death.

"I got you. Your alright" Greyson whispered.

He held her tightly. "Your alright." He repeated.

"We are going to get her I promise you. Even Blake said himself she is our number one priority. She is going to be fine."

I hope she is Greyson thought.

Lila nodded even though she knew that wasn't true despite how much she hoped it was.

Blake overheard their conversation and walked back to his office. He didn't know how to feel about anything. His life is like a game of chess he has only two moves he can make and they both end up in the enemy saying "check mate."

"Your doing the right thing." Isabella reassured him.

"Really?" Blake hesitated in asking but he had to, "Its all going to hell isn't it Bella."

She looked up from the ground staring into his bright blue eyes Isabella felt her heart breaking at their ending.

"Blake neither of us can decide what the future holds. Our fate is not permanent nothing is." Isabella left the room leaving him to his thoughts.

There was only one thing they needed for their plan to work, the girl who was just out of reach from their grasp. Time will tell if they succeed but their chances are left up to fate.

Acknowledgements

First and foremost, I want to thank my family for all their support, especially mam, dad, Francesca, Gemma and grandad who helped this book become reality.

I want to thank all my English teachers and my head of year who have taught me and encouraged me to keep going.

I want to thank my three closest friends Obi, Chloe and Julia thank you for the overwhelming love and support I love you guys.

I would also like to thank primary school Mrs Storey who was the first teacher that made me fall in love with English and reading.

I would like to thank Ian Balmain without you the book would definitely not be finished without your amazing editing skills thank you.

Lastly, I would like to thank everyone who has taken the time to read this book, I have put so much effort and time into this story I hope you love this world as much as I do.

Printed in Great Britain
by Amazon